She was in a small low-ceilinged place. There were scattered groups of pulsating red and green lights, a low hum of electrical machinery. Then her eyes adjusted and she saw the face.

It was a man, pale, gaunt, hair close-cropped and thin, eyes dark sunken hollows. He stared intently back at her.

Was it John?

She said his name. A whisper. There was no answer.

He didn't move. Three slender curved rods of polished steel seemed to hold him rigid. They curved out and down, then, to join upright chrome poles projecting from some sort of massive console below, its polished steel and chrome broken by dials and switches.

A coldness rose in Susan, an unspeakable horror. She wanted to run, couldn't.

She heard him say, "You shouldn't have come." The voice was electronic, a monotone. "Or worked here. Ever." A bitter tone suddenly. "Go. Go and forget everything—what I am, what you've seen. Go and forget. Now."

HEADS

David Osborn

BANTAM BOOKS
TORONTO · NEW YORK · LONDON · SYDNEY · AUCKLAND

HEADS

A Bantam Book / May 1985

ISBN 0-553-23869-8

Published simultaneously in the United States and Canada

Bantam Books are published by Bantam Books, Inc. Its
trademark, consisting of the words "Bantam Books" and the
portrayal of a rooster, is Registered in U.S. Patent and Trademark Office and in other countries. Marca Registrada. Bantam
Books, Inc., 666 Fifth Avenue, New York, New York 10103.

To Robin,
with love

Prologue

Nighttime. The faint smell of antiseptic. The hospital's p.a. system a muted whisper into light-dimmed corridors, nurses' stations silent islands. The occasional medical figure, uniform starch-white, white shoes crepe-soled silent.

The man in Room 203 in the West Wing was dying of cancer of the pancreas, which had spread to his liver. Neither radiation therapy nor chemotherapy had been able to halt the carcinoma's relentless progress. He had a week to live. At best.

And knew it. This morning, he'd been moved to a private room. He was bone-gaunt, his hair thinned almost to nothing and lifeless. His skin was yellow and his hollow eyes were dull with hopeless resignation. All afternoon, he'd stared out at the fading green of September trees on the hospital lawn, wishing it were October so he could see the leaves changing to red and gold a final time.

He didn't recognize the doctor when he came in.

Nor the woman, apparently also a doctor from her white coat and the stethoscope thrust casually into a side pocket. He'd never seen either before.

The doctor pulled a chair close to the bed. He was relatively young and exceptionally good-looking in a lean and masculine way, with deep-set intelligent eyes and a strong face. His manner was quiet; he looked tired and overworked. The woman, also young and looking equally tired, stood back, respectful and attentive. She was slender and quite beautiful, actually, with delicate features and amber eyes, and had titian hair swept back into a loose chignon. The soft aroma of her perfume reached the dying man. For an instant his eyes rested on the gentle swell of her bosom beneath her white coat. She was life where he was death.

The doctor introduced himself. "I'm Dr. Michael Burgess. This is my associate, Katherine Blair. We're with the Borg-Harrison Foundation research lab in Bethesda. Can we talk a moment?"

Without waiting for an answer, Michael opened a folder containing biographical information. The dying man had an IQ of 138, a master's degree in social anthropology, a doctorate in political science. He was going to leave behind a wife of twenty years and two daughters in their teens. He perfectly fitted their research needs.

Michael pretended to study the material, although he'd gone over it many times. It was to give the dying man a chance to get used to him, although usually the magic name Borg-Harrison put potential volunteers at ease. Presently he said, "I know you know how sick you are so I'll come directly to the point. What would you say if I offered you a better-than-even chance to live at least another two or three years?"

The dying man looked back blankly. Michael was used to that; they all did. He said, "Do you understand me? We are quite certain we can keep you alive."

The hollow eyes flickered with sudden anger. "Is this some sort of joke?"

Michael rose to look out the window. Occasional streetlamps made islands of pale light amid the dark shadowed lawns and trees surrounding the hospital. He said, "Hardly. Although I have to tell you that you would no longer be mobile, not the way you are now, able to get up and move about. You would have no further uncontrollable pain, however, and you'd be able to keep up with the world, converse with friends, read." He smiled and gestured at the silent television set he was certain the man never watched. "Share other people's lives. We're running a brain-research program in which we'd isolate your body and your cancer from your brain in a neurological blocking process which prevents the cancer from metastasizing."

There was more, but he usually tried to stop there. With the layman you had to be careful. You could only go so far. Occasionally one would ask about food and he'd tell them they'd receive everything they needed through total parenteral nutrition, amino acids, glucose, proteins, minerals, insulin, all dripped into a main artery at the rate of twenty drops per minute.

This one didn't ask anything else. He was too concerned with his death. He said, "It sounds like medical double-talk." But the anger was gone now, the tone different.

Michael recognized the change. The patient suddenly wanted to believe. "I'm sure it must," he admitted. "But who knew a few years ago they'd be able to create human life in test tubes?"

The hollow eyes focused on him again. "Okay, but why me as one of your guinea pigs? That's what you're saying I'd be, aren't you? An experiment? There are thousands like me and you can't have had much success. I've never heard of this and in the last year I've read nearly everything going in medicine."

Michael knew the speech had taken enormous effort. The man had to feel nauseated, desperately ill throughout his whole body and numb with the drugs he'd been given to combat agonizing pain. Talking at all, even saying just a few words, had to be nearly impossible for him.

"Two reasons," he replied. "First, we only accept people on the verge of death. Second, the program is limited and under certain government security restrictions. Where you personally are concerned, to be frank, it was pure chance. You came up on an interhospital computer."

For the first time Katherine Blair spoke. Her voice was softly authoritative. "Your chances are over eighty percent in your favor. If we move immediately."

The dying man saw her exchange a look with the

doctor. She seemed to hesitate. "Well, go on," he said. "You may have time, I don't."

He wondered fleetingly if in spite of his professional assurance, the woman might be stronger than Burgess, more pragmatic to complement his possibly greater idealism. Or perhaps more ambitious. In a quiet way she almost seemed in charge.

Michael said, "Okay, here it is. If you agree to this, you won't be able to see your family again. Or current friends. Ever. You will have donated your 'remains' to science and they'll be told you died and will be given a sealed coffin."

He got the reaction he always got. Breath-held silence. Eyes wide with shock. The thought of immediate and irrevocable separation left all of them as frightened as of death itself.

But almost at once he could see some of the blow ebb and a glimmer of hope reappear. Again from experience, he could guess the dying man's thoughts. Stay alive for another two years, and who could know what might happen? Perhaps, finally, a cure for cancer.

It was exactly what the man was thinking. He glanced at the woman doctor. The smile she gave him was filled with care. He suddenly felt safe with her.

"When would it happen?" he asked. "Is it surgery? or what?"

"Some of it is surgery," she replied. She was closer now and put her hand over his. Her touch was cool. "And if we do it at all it's got to be immediately, tonight. You're going to need all the

DAVID OSBORN

strength possible, and from now on you go down-hill like a toboggan."

Something hard like iron grabbed at his heart. Again, his breath wouldn't come. Or words. Tonight? No! It was impossible. He tried to think. Death was right there. A dark presence just by his bed, the awful terror of not *being* anymore, the black non-knowing forever. No words could describe it. Every dawn now he poured sweat and stifled screams. And prayed for a coma. He didn't want to know the final moment.

He said, "Whenever you want."

Michael nodded and took a printed form from the folder. "I'll need your signature."

He didn't read it. What was the point? Besides, Borg-Harrison was a prestigious organization. Its chairman, Admiral Walter Burnleigh, was a friend of the President of the United States. There could be nothing fraudulent or unethical here. He scrawled his signature with Michael's pen, boldly, because he knew if he wasn't defiant he'd go to pieces.

He asked, "When will my wife hear?" He felt a wave of heartbreak for the past, for what might have been.

"In the morning. You will have died in your sleep. You won't have suffered. In a way, she'll be grateful and happy for you."

He felt the sting of tears.

Michael rose. "We'll be back in an hour."

The warm pressure of his hand, his quiet smile. The door closed behind him and Katherine Blair.

6

Only a trace of her perfume lingered to say they'd ever been there.

It was done. Minutes ago there'd been nothing but the black despair of inexorable injustice, the inevitability of death. Why? Why him? Now, suddenly, there was hope.

A nurse gave him a shot. He thought of his wife again, her love and courage. Hiding her agony. To end her misery tonight was a last thing he could do for her. He thought of his daughters; the lives before them. He'd given up hope that he'd ever know of their accomplishments and dreams: college, young men, weddings, grandchildren.

But now, possibly, he would.

He stared at the dark rectangle that was the night window of his room. It was as though death had been sent to wait outside. He ceased thinking about others, then. He began to think only of himself. He didn't have to die. He might live. He just might.

He felt as though a miracle had happened.

Pretty soon, some nurses came with a stretcher to take him away.

1

John Flemming was a tall, lean, tousle-haired, slightly eccentric genius from an old Main Line Philadelphia family, a heritage he preferred to disavow as antidemocratic.

As the youngest-ever medical director of the University Hospital Brain Research Laboratory in Washington, he had recently been mentioned as a possible Nobel candidate for his work in connection with neurometrics, a highly complex computer technique in which brain waves read by standard electroencephalogram were computer-analyzed and compared against statistical norms in a way that enabled diagnosis of a score of diseases with deadly accuracy.

John shared a rented and sagging old frame house on tree-lined Sixth Street behind the Library of Congress with Susan McCullough, his assistant and a graduate student in neurophysiology from the Midwest. A year ago she had suddenly announced she was moving in with him. She had decided that underneath an often cynical and chauvinistic exterior there was a man she badly wanted to marry.

Tonight they were giving a party to celebrate the fact that they had finally raised enough money to buy the house. They had come home early from the Lab, a collection of cast-off garret rooms in the hospital's oldest building, where paint peeled and worn desks were littered with books, papers, and computer terminals. Susan had put on tight-fitting jeans, espadrilles, and a fancifully embroidered peasant blouse that complemented her dark hair and sea-green eyes and her slender full-bosomed body with its long leggy casual look. She had made spaghetti alla carbonara, garlic bread, and salad. John had changed into fresh khakis and sneakers and loped down to the local liquor store to return with jugs of Chianti and Chablis.

The party was a huge success, attended by a small mob of fellow medical scientists, some doctors like John, others grad students like Susan. Three of John's classmates from Harvard Medical School also showed. Along with John, they were planning to attend a Saturday workshop in brain research at Johns Hopkins in Baltimore.

The September heat wave was still stifling Washington. People sat out on the front stoop or filled the backyard. John chained Percival, his oversized, overfriendly dog, to his doghouse and Percy lay in it all evening, panting, with only his enormous black head and mournful eyes showing in the doorway.

There was a problem, though. The host and hostess had had a hell of a row an hour before the party and weren't speaking.

The cause was an unfortunate pop-magazine article on brain research.

The article itself was inoffensive enough. The writer had merely said things professionals knew all too well but of which the public was largely ignorant. He had likened the human brain to a vast uncharted sea and asked what its potential might be if when using only about five to ten percent of its cells, mankind had already harnessed electricity and the atom, mastered both sea and air, and created complex legal and social systems as well as art, music, and literature awesome in their beauty.

But in a more personal vein he'd written things flattering to Susan at John's expense. Under a rather sexy picture of her—there was no picture of John— he'd said, "Presiding over the outstanding genius of Dr. Flemming is Susan McCullough, a rare beauty in the usually frumpy scientific community who calmly brings order to the lab's otherwise chaos."

John was proud of the Lab and his leadership of it, and although he hadn't admitted it, Susan knew the statement had really irked him. He'd taken it out on her by griping about a test he claimed she'd made a mess of. She'd fought back because it wasn't her fault. A week of eighty hours' hard work in a heat wave had taken its toll. By the time the guests arrived, the host and hostess weren't speaking to each other and something had to give.

The big blow came about ten-thirty. Emerging from the kitchen with a large pitcher of iced Chablis,

Susan found John holding forth on his favorite topic—Medicine and Science, both used far too often for their own sake and not for people. The most forgotten words in the medical dictionary were "human" and "being," he'd always said. Medical advances cloaked in mumbo-jumbo and secrecy enraged him.

He'd cornered one of their guests, Michael Burgess, who was an old colleague and a neurosurgeon doing brain research for the Borg-Harrison Foundation. John was hammering away at Michael for "being so goddamned hush-hush." Michael, a biology whiz kid from way back in high school, and brilliantly innovative both in med school and residency, had deeply disappointed John by "disappearing" for nearly five years behind a screen of secrecy.

"I don't know what the hell you're doing, Michael," Susan heard John say, "so what's the point of it? Or will someone be kind enough to tell us ninety-nine statutory years from now?"

She stopped. John's mildly eccentric manner had changed to that of a zealot. He was flapping his arms, his voice was raised. Susan wondered how many drinks he'd had.

"Secrecy is like lies," he went on. "And you know it. You start off with a few little white ones and end up murdering the truth everywhere. And in your case, my friend, probably doing things medicine shouldn't be doing at all. If Borg-Harrison can't make your work public, then it's either some damned anti-people covert nonsense for the Pentagon or it's science for science's sake, which amounts to the same thing. And if you don't think so, you're still as naive as Susan, who believes you guys never operate when you don't have to."

That did it. All right, she was naive, and so what! She paused mid-stride, opened her mouth to protest, took in the superior, slightly triumphant expression he wore, and changed her mind. Words would get her nowhere. Only action would. Without a second thought, she dumped the whole jug of iced wine over his head. "Don't look now," she said, "but your soapbox is about to float out to sea."

She ought to have known John would be hurt instead of angry. Wine ran down his surprised sensitive face. He turned and went silently upstairs. She called after him to say she was sorry—and meant it—but he didn't answer.

Michael laughed and shook his head. "Don't let us upset you, Susan. Ultimately John and I have pretty much the same goals, I suspect."

She didn't see John again all evening. Guests had fun talking about what she'd done, then forgot about it. When everyone had gone, however, she began to look for him and couldn't find him anywhere.

In the backyard, Percival had come out of his doghouse, all one hundred and seventy pounds of him. He was half Newfoundland and probably half horse, John always said. He'd brought Percival home from the pound one day, fully grown. "They had him in a cage only this big!" he'd said indignantly. He and Percival were instant soul mates.

Percival whined. "What's the matter, Percy?" Susan stroked his huge head and peered around the yard. Why was the dog so restless?

That's when she felt whatever it was on her leg. Something crawling. Silent. Her mind stopped. Her innards froze. She had just registered that it was a human hand when it slithered back down her calf from her knee to her ankle and clamped hard.

The scream got halfway up her throat to her lips.

A familiar voice said, "Come on in. I've got everything we need."

John. She tried to get words out. Nothing came. Her legs were jelly.

A match flared. A candle flickered. She looked. He was in the doghouse. He'd built it huge for Percival; there was enough room for two Newfoundlands. He'd spread out a blanket, had a bottle of champagne in an ice bucket and two glasses. He raised one. It sparkled. "Here's to my residence in the correct place."

"You idiot. We both should be in it." She joined him.

The floor was hard. The confined space smelled ferociously of dog. The candle made it terribly hot, and once or twice Susan felt fleas nip. Eventually, after they'd drunk all the champagne, she persuaded John to come back to the house, where she stretched out gratefully on the smooth percale sheets of their old brass bed.

Just before she fell asleep, she thought: Oh, my God, I'm going to marry one of those mad scientists. There was laughter in her dreams.

In the morning, when she'd showered and was

brushing her teeth, she smelled coffee. She wrapped a towel around her waist and went downstairs. She found John in the kitchen. He'd already started beating eggs, toast was in the toaster. He had on a T-shirt and baggy boxer shorts and looked all spindly-legged, unshaven, and ghastly. He had to have a colossal hangover.

"Why don't you let me do that?"

"I can manage. Sit down." Authoritative.

Susan hid a smile, got the newspaper from the front stoop.

They ate in silence. John studied the front page. Susan suddenly realized that he was scratching himself. Presently, eyes serious, he put down his coffee, gravely pulled something invisible from his armpit, and held it up for inspection.

In seconds they were both doubled over. She went and sat on his lap and put her arms around his neck. "Maniac! I love you."

"I love you." He kissed her. "I think I'll go drown a few fleas," he said.

He left for the brain-research workshop in Baltimore twenty minutes later with a promise to be back by six-thirty, in time for an early movie.

He stopped on the front steps, going out, and unexpectedly turned and said, "Besides saying you were beautiful, Susan, the guy was right about something else. He was right about your bringing calm to chaos and your presiding over me. If it weren't for you, I don't think any of us at the Lab would ever get a damn thing done. I certainly wouldn't."

Susan's eyes misted. She could barely see him

14

amble across the street to their car. She watched him slide in behind the steering wheel. That dear sweet gangling body—sometimes it looked as though it were still in its teens.

She had no way of knowing she'd never see it that way again.

2

The accident occurred at precisely six-twelve. The exact location was the Maryland Route 197 exit on the Baltimore–Washington Parkway about twenty miles north of the capital. The weather was clear, the road dry.

John had left Baltimore earlier than he'd planned. Except for reliving old times with his Harvard friends, the day had turned out to be disappointing. He'd learned nothing new in the workshop and spent most of the time thinking of Susan and remembering last night.

With his mind somewhere else, he was driving at only fifty, perhaps not fast enough for the heavy Saturday traffic on the Parkway.

He was in the right lane and southbound when the road started to widen preparatory to becoming an exit ramp down to Route 197, which traversed beneath it. By the time he woke up to where he was going, there was only just time to swerve left back onto the Parkway itself.

He flashed a glance in his rear mirror and missed seeing the heavy Buick sedan bearing down on his left-rear at sixty-five. A scream of tires and the Buick's right-front slammed into him. The Honda slewed diagonally and smashed up against the high curb that separated the Parkway from the descending exit ramp. The impact threw it into the air. It hit a utility pole, crashed down onto the ramp, and then, on its side and still moving fast, slammed, roof-first, against the rear of a Ford station wagon. The Ford catapulted forward. The Honda, now upside down, slid a dozen yards more and stopped. A flicker of light and its gas tank blew up.

From beginning to end, the accident took about six seconds.

Above, on the Parkway, the Buick had caromed against a Chevrolet in the left lane, but both drivers managed to control their vehicles. There were three minor nose-to-tail collisions among cars coming up behind as a stream of tailgating traffic skidded all over the road trying to stop.

On the ramp, beyond the Honda, it was another story. The blow from the Honda whiplashed the Ford driver and stunned him. The Ford shot out of control onto Route 197, where it was hit by a five-ton GM dump truck. The truck was relatively unharmed. The whole front of the Ford, including motor, dashboard, and steering wheel, was torn away. The driver had both legs broken as well as his nose and jaw, and was severely cut. A safety belt kept him from being hurtled headfirst into the road and probably killed.

Then nothing at all happened for about twenty seconds. There was eerie silence.

The first movement came from the truck driver. He was a young man and he leapt down and sprinted to the Ford. His mind didn't go farther than the slumped figure of the driver, a gray-haired man whose exposed legs were beginning to rush blood.

The first person to register John was the middle-aged woman driver of a Pontiac Firebird who had used the exit ramp as an escape route to avoid a collision. She got out of her car, shaking, and looked down the ramp. The Honda's roof was crushed flat to its doors and hood. John's head and shoulders and one arm extended outside it. Pinned by the roof, his face was downward on the glass- and oil-strewn ramp. He was apparently conscious. She saw his arm move. The Honda's whole rear was an inferno but the driver was still protected by the jammed-up front and back seats.

The woman kept her head and finally found a fire extinguisher eight cars back up the Parkway. It was pathetically small, only five pounds. When she and a man got close enough to squirt it, it seemed to empty out in seconds and do no good at all. She ran to find another.

Several minutes went by. The Honda's seats began to burn. Men had gathered and tried to roll the car upright, but the heat was now too intense.

John began to burn. And scream. His mouth opened against the cement pavement, his eyes bulged. His screams became continuous and horrifying. Some people couldn't take it and turned away.

There was a gas station a hundred yards down Route 197 and the attendant had called the Emergency Central number the moment the accident happened.

The ambulance made it before the police. It came from the Thomas Benton Memorial Hospital near the town of Laurel, three miles away, and took six minutes. The police took six and a half. They were Highway Patrol, Maryland state troopers.

There were two emergency medical technicians in the ambulance as well as the driver. The word was that the accident was bad and they were still pulling away from the hospital when one had the foresight to ask the Emergency Medical Center for a patch. That meant a continuous open radio line to their own emergency room at Thomas Benton.

They came down 197 to the accident, and since the Honda was still upside down and burning, they took care of the Ford driver first, letting the police go to work on the Honda fire with fifty-pound chemical extinguishers. When they had immobilized both the driver's legs with inflatable splints, they stretchered and covered him, checked his vital signs, gave him seventy-five milligrams of Demerol, and put the stretcher in the ambulance. The driver administered oxygen, established an IV, an intravenous line, for plasma, and began compressing several bad head cuts.

The two EMTs now ran for the Honda. A Laurel Fire Department emergency truck had arrived. It took care of whatever fire the police couldn't and poured water over the carcass to cool it. Firemen wearing heavy asbestos gloves turned the car right-side-up and went to work on the jammed door and roof of John's side with a hydraulic "jaws of life." It took only three minutes to cut through and extricate him.

When they saw John's body, no one in the crowd of drivers from the Parkway tried to get any closer than he was. John's body was black from the chest down and smelled like burned fat. One of his feet was nearly gone, with just charred bone showing. He was conscious but confused, and in such serious shock as not to feel much pain.

The EMTs didn't waste any time. They got him into the ambulance, put an oxygen cone on his face, and headed for Thomas Benton. On the way they radioed his condition.

"Sixty percent third-, twenty percent second-degree burns on his body. Left foot gone. Vital signs, pulse one-sixty, blood pressure eighty over zero, palpable. Breathing forty a minute. He's tachycardic and hypotensive."

The emergency-room resident told them to hold the Demerol. With a blood pressure that low, it could kill him. He also told them to try to establish an IV line and begin a lactated Ringer's solution, as much as the IV line would handle.

"We'll try, but he's a mess."

"How are his lungs?"

"Still clear. He has no head or facial burns."

The ambulance made it back to Thomas Benton

in five minutes. They wheeled John and the Ford victim into Emergency. There was a young intern, just out of medical school, the resident, and three nurses. Two nurses were veterans, one was young and inexperienced. When she saw John, she began to cry. The senior nurse sent her with the intern to take care of the Ford driver.

The resident at once put an oxygen mask on John to try to stave off pulmonary edema. Then he and the senior nurse immediately began removing John's clothes, carefully scissoring them away where they had stuck to burned flesh.

Before John arrived, the resident had called down a respiratory therapist to take a blood gas. A calm, gray-haired woman, she quickly got a needle into an upper-arm artery, took blood, and sent a lab technician who'd come with her rushing off with a syringe.

The ambulance EMTs hadn't had time to establish an IV and when the therapist was finished the senior nurse helped the resident establish intercaths into the large veins under both left and right clavicles. They had to cut away some charred skin before they could get the intercath in the left side. The moment this was done, the nurse then poled bottles of Ringer's solution and adjusted the clamps for a 1000-cc drip.

"Put him in Trendelenburg." That meant raising his knees, lowering his head, an anti-shock measure.

They kept him on three liters of oxygen. In five minutes they had the blood-gas result. The resident glanced over it quickly. The reading was normal but pulmonary complications would be bound to set in soon. He ordered the second nurse to administer two amps of sodium bicarbonate through the IV and told her when she was finished to run John's current data and prognosis up on the ER computer. Clerical would take it off in the morning for the record. He told her also to notify the hospital chaplain.

An X-ray technician came in with a portable machine to take chest X rays, and while he was doing it, the resident went to check the Ford driver. When he saw the intern was making out all right on his own and that the young nurse had herself under control, he returned to John and studied him a moment. An amputation of the left leg below the knee was clearly indicated, but there was no point in getting together a surgical team. There wasn't time. The burn unit at the Lincoln Medical Center in the District of Columbia had been alerted and a helicopter was on its way.

The senior nurse sponged John's forehead. His eyes pleaded. Not so much to stop the pain—he still wasn't feeling that much. But to end his confusion, to tell him what had happened, where he was.

"You're going to be okay, fella. Just take it easy. You've had a serious accident but we'll have you fixed up in no time."

The senior nurse had prepared a catheter and she and the resident now began very gently to cut away remaining charred material from John's genitals, where gasoline had seeped all around before igniting. It was the only way to get it off without ripping out chunks of flesh from his lower abdomen and from what remained of his penis. They had to establish immediate drainage from his bladder.

Once, their eyes met. They both knew everything they were doing had to be done because they were in medicine. But they also knew it was probably a waste of time.

3

Susan had been preparing dinner and watching the clock. John was already an hour late and she debated whether to call Johns Hopkins and try to find someone who might know when he'd left.

The ringing telephone shattered the kitchen's silence and gave her a start. For a moment she just stared. Then she picked up the receiver.

"Is this John Flemming's residence?"

"Yes."

"Miss McCullough?"

She sensed immediately that it might be bad simply because the voice was a stranger's. Her heart leapt. "Yes."

A name she didn't catch, Reverend someone. "I'm the chaplain at the Thomas Benton Hospital."

Oh, God, no, no. Chaplains didn't call unless someone had died.

"I'm afraid there's been a serious accident."

A blinding image; then, remembrance. The long-

24

buried past rushing to the raw present. Another phone, one on a wall, its bell jangling the silence of a farmhouse kitchen, the receiver-distant Midwestern drawl of some sheriff's deputy, callous. "We got a couple of automobile fatalities here. Pair by the name of McCullough. Can someone come up and identify them?"

The phone hanging unanswered at the end of its black cord. Her dazed walk through the creaking screen door into the dry August dust of the barren front yard, stray chickens scattering before bare feet and child-thin legs.

And now John. Her whole life. Oh, please, not again. Please.

"John?"

"Yes. A collision with another car, Miss McCullough, about forty minutes ago."

"He's dead?"

A hesitation. Then, "No. But he's not very well. He's being transferred now by helicopter to the burn unit at the Lincoln Medical Center."

Rising panic. She fought it back.

"I'll go right away."

"Perhaps you shouldn't drive right now, Miss McCullough. Can you get someone to take you?"

She tried to think, couldn't. "No. I don't know."

Thirty minutes later, he was there, an inconspicuous older man with kind and worried eyes. She was wearing jeans and moccasins and a white shirt. She didn't think to change or do anything with her hair. She grabbed an old cardigan and her handbag and went out to his car with him.

He drove so carefully to the Medical Center she wanted to scream.

"Could we go a little faster?"

"Of course."

But they didn't. They crawled through Washington traffic. Please live, John. Please. Don't you die, too. Not the morgue again and a sheet pulled back from a smashed body—"Yes, sir, that's her." Not the awful unbearable aloneness and relatives making it worse by pretending to care.

It seemed forever before the grounds and building of the Medical Center appeared. Then it took time to locate John. For some unexplained reason, Reception hadn't yet been notified he was there. She was given a ward number, there were endless sterile hospital corridors and nurses' stations, directions asked and given almost reluctantly by uninterested white-uniformed personnel.

She finally found the correct place, a room that smelled badly of dead flesh and burned tissue. There were six beds, two of which were hidden by drawn curtains. They wouldn't let her in without protective sterile clothing, a surgical cap and gown and mask. But it didn't make any difference, John wasn't there. She was told he was being debrided in a special antiseptic-bath facility, "floating off bacteria and burned tissue." He wouldn't be back for an hour. That casual.

Down the hall, she found a waiting area with chairs and some magazines. She tried to read, slowly turning the pages of one magazine after another. Nothing registered.

She saw only John. And herself. Their life together. Last night at the party. This morning in their kitchen.

"I love you, you maniac!"

"I love you."

She kept falling asleep. Waking. Going back to see if he was there.

Returning to her chair and magazines.

Nine o'clock, ten. Two hours. Not one.

Sitting on a hard chair she was once again in the sheriff's office. Questions:

"Did your old man drink?" "What grade you in, kid, fifth?" "Got a uncle or a aunt or someone we can call?"

An orderly passed by.

"Could you please tell me where I can get some coffee?"

"Sorry, miss. The canteen is closed."

Suddenly a stretcher was being wheeled into the ward, a white cluster of nurses and IV poles. She tried to follow it.

"I'm sorry. You can't come in here."

Say something. Quickly. Whatever they needed to hear. Tell them you're Mrs. Flemming. Her dry lips tried to form words. She tried to see through a gap in the curtains they'd drawn around the stretcher.

"Susan?"

She turned. A familiar figure, dark hair, tall. For an instant in her shocked impression, it was John. It took several seconds for her to fit the face into the present. Then she remembered last night and the party. It was Michael Burgess.

"I'm a consultant neurosurgeon here, Susan. I just

happened to have been called over on another case. I'm so awfully sorry."

He told the nurses to let her be with John. "I'm going upstairs," he said. "He's due for some skin grafting but he's started having pulmonary problems. I want to talk to his doctor."

She was given a mask and gown and went to John alone. She was very frightened. It was even harder to understand what she saw, to accept. What had she imagined? A pale bandaged John? A fragile long form gently covered with a white sheet? Gaunt, tired eyes, unshaven cheeks?

There must be some mistake. That bloated raw red flesh on a stryker frame wasn't John, couldn't be. John was all wonderful ribs and bones with tangles of hair on his stomach and chest and beneath it tawny skin like old unpolished marble. This man was naked, his few patches of unburned skin and the sheet beneath him blackened by silver nitrate. He was getting oxygen through nasal prongs, one leg was gone below the knee and there were drains and a catheter in the truncated blob of formless flesh that had been his penis.

A darkness came into Susan's eyes. She thought: I'm going to faint. But she didn't. She forced herself to concentrate on John's face.

"John?"

Feverish eyes turned to her. Swollen cracked lips muttered, "You shouldn't have come."

"It's all right."

A long silence. Then, "The car must be a write-off."

"It's insured. Don't try to talk."

"What did you do with Percy?"

"He's tied up. Someone's coming over to feed him."

It wasn't true. She'd forgotten about Percy. Left alone too long, he howled. But it didn't matter.

A nurse appeared. Stiff. Authoritative. "I think that's all he can take right now."

"Can't I just sit here?"

John's eyes had closed. They flicked open. "She stays. It's my goddamned life. Don't go, Susan. Don't."

Susan heard the change in his breathing. It rattled hoarsely and he coughed. His lungs were filling with water. It terrified her.

One unburned hand fumbled feebly, looking for hers. Susan took it. Defied, the nurse left in cold silence.

John's eyes closed again. Susan bowed her head in case he should open them and see her crying.

After a while, Michael came back and beckoned her out into the hall so they could talk. She gently released her hand from John's and went to join him.

He said, "They're going to risk some skin grafting to help protect him against infection. But they'll let him rest a little first and try to lessen his pulmonary edema. I have things to take care of. Will you be all right?"

"I'll manage."

"Has anyone given you anything?"

The question surprised her. Given her what? She told him she didn't understand.

"Anything to help you. Maybe some Valium."

She felt a flush of anger. She wasn't going to

depend on pills and drugs to get her through John's hell. She started to put ice into her reply but the concern in his expression stopped her and she remembered that he was a friend. He had to be upset, too. She rested her hand on his arm. "Thank you, Michael. Very much. But I don't need it."

"I think you do," he said.

He took her arm and she found herself powerless to resist. He walked her to the nurse's station and asked for a ten-milligram Valium. The duty nurse smiled. "We're on unit-dose medication, Doctor, but I think I can find you some." She got her handbag from the counter, rummaged in it, and came up with her own small prescription bottle. Michael accepted a tablet, and got Susan a cup of water from a water cooler.

She took the Valium, and glancing at him then, knew he'd answer honestly the question she had to ask.

She said, "He's not going to live, is he?"

"No," he said. "I don't think he will. I'm sorry."

"Why will they bother him with grafting?"

"They have to try everything possible. You wouldn't want them not to."

"No," she said slowly. "I guess not." They started back toward John's room. "I'll sit with him until they come," she said. "Is there any chance you could go to the operating room with him? So he's not alone?"

"Of course."

They went into John's room, then Michael disappeared. Susan sat silently. As she listened to John's hoarse, labored breathing, she thought about their life together, what they'd had, what they'd wanted to have. She kept her eyes on his face and once in a while gently touched his forehead.

At five A.M. they came to get him. One of the nurses told her Dr. Burgess was waiting in OR. John opened his eyes and recognized her.

"They're going to graft some skin, John."

"That makes sense." His voice was thin, like a child's.

"Michael Burgess will be there."

"Michael?"

"He heard about you and came over."

A faint smile. "Left his damn secrets for me?"

"And I'll be here when you come down."

She went with him to the elevator surrounded by a phalanx of nurses. When the doors opened, she knew she was going to cry. Don't, Susan, she thought, don't. You've got to keep up the sham. Got to. She smiled and kissed his forehead. "I love you, John."

He said suddenly and quite clearly, "Susan, listen, I love you too, I love you more than anything in the world." His eyes were bright and clear.

It was more than she could bear. She started after him. They mustn't take him from her. Ever. But she was too late. The elevator doors closed in on his stretcher.

She went back to the waiting area to leaf once more through one magazine after another. She tried not to imagine John and what they were doing to him. Time seemed forever.

After a while she just sat, numb.

"You can go home now, kid. The deputy here will drive you. Your cousins said they'd be by tomorrow."

The empty front yard, the silent house. The bare kitchen. There was only the old farm dog, half-blind. The telephone receiver still dangled on its cord.

Michael Burgess had been standing in front of her for some moments before she realized he was there. His expression told her immediately. She stood up.

"He's gone?"

"Yes. I'm sorry. We really didn't expect it so soon."

"Did he know?"

"No. He was asleep."

"Can I see him?"

"Susan, he left various organs to medicine. Tomorrow would be better. In the chapel."

They walked to John's room so she could get whatever of his things hadn't burned, his briefcase, his wallet and keys. Someone had already wrapped them in a package. A taxi was waiting for her downstairs. Michael had ordered one. She said good-bye to him and thanked him for everything. The day was bright and sunny. People came and went. People who didn't know. She felt a strange detachment from it all. Nothing seemed real.

She went home and fed Percy. And herself. She reached John's mother and told her.

Then she went to bed. There would be time to make arrangements with an undertaker tomorrow, to notify other people, his friends, colleagues. Now she had to sleep.

Late in the evening when she awoke, she went down to the kitchen and made coffee and sat without drinking it at the kitchen table, first closing the windows because the heat wave had finally broken and the night was unexpectedly chilly.

Reality slowly returned. The coffee grew cold and bitter. The kitchen light glared. It was dark and silent outside.

She'd spent the night alone in the farmhouse before relatives came and took her away. It seemed so terribly long ago, her childhood, and yet just yesterday.

That night, too, she'd sat and listened to the sound of the kitchen clock ticking away time. She sipped her cold coffee and heartbreak finally came.

4

A week after John's funeral, Susan threw herself back into work. John's diagnostic project was extensive and she found another grad student to help her compile the many files of random notes he had left behind. It would be a long job. The notes were typically John, lacking continuity in content as well as in time. Recipes for some obscure way to dish up coq au vin would be mixed in with ideas on a new mathematical formula or with a rambling critique of a Kennedy Center concert. John's hand was spidery and small. He didn't use sentences and more often than not left out all verbs. Deciphering page after page of jumbled thoughts often came close to cryptography.

The work helped ease a sense of loss which sometimes nearly overwhelmed her. Nighttime was the hardest. There were things she wanted not to remember. She'd never been able to see John's body because the coroner had sealed the coffin, the rule with organ donors. Then, there was the kind of formal funeral John would have detested: a minister too young to understand the words of the wise old men he read so glibly from the Bible; John's mother, the center of attraction after being rejected so long by her son; herself, ignored by his family and made to feel an intruder because even though they'd shared bed, board, and their bodies, she and John hadn't been married or even officially engaged.

Afterward, John's mother had coldly reclaimed most of the antiques she'd loaned her son and there'd been Percy to find a home for. She couldn't handle him alone, or the memories his mournful eyes evoked.

Throughout, Michael Burgess was wonderfully supportive and helpful. One cold December morning he called to ask her to dinner and she accepted gratefully. He picked her up and they drove to a small French restaurant in Georgetown where the street was cobbled and the gnarled winter-bare branches of huge trees met overhead. It was an intimate and charming place. Michael knew the chef and she listened delighted as they arranged a dinner and accompanying wine with her particular tastes wholly in mind. Then, while they ate, Michael gently questioned her about her academic and professional background.

"You went to Harvard?"

"Yes."

"From a Midwest high school? That's not easy to do! What did you major in?"

"I doubled. Biology and biochemistry."

"And then took your master's at Johns Hopkins?"

"Yes. In neurobiology. How do you know so much?"

"Ah," he said mysteriously. "And after that you did half your doctorate at Stanford. Neurophysiology."

"Yes. The other half is ongoing at University Hospital. I keep delaying my thesis—it will be on neurometrics. I really should have turned it in two years ago but I've been so busy."

"Where's home, your family?"

"Don't laugh. It was Oneida, South Dakota. My father had a chicken farm. But he and my mother both died when I was very young." She managed a smile. "A car crash."

"That's terrible. I'm sorry. Who paid all the school then?"

"The chicken farm was sold. And I worked and got scholarships."

He was quiet a moment. Susan waited. Somehow she had the impression he really wasn't that interested in her academic background, even though a lot of people seemed to think it was pretty outstanding.

She heard him say, "I guess I was lucky. I always had everything, whatever I wanted—premed, medical school. When I was a kid I was fascinated by surgery. My mother bought me fish endlessly until I got into rodents. Then she filled the house with rats. Perfection became compulsive with me."

He stirred his coffee and then suddenly looked at her and said, "But to hell with that. I've got something more important in mind. How would you like to come to work for us at Borg-Harrison?"

It didn't catch her that much by surprise. She'd

begun to suspect. She tried to think how to answer. She wouldn't finish up John's work for some time, and being at the University Hospital Lab gave her a sense of security she badly needed at the moment. But there would come a day eventually, she knew, when John's work was finally off her desk and the Lab might not need her anymore.

She told Michael she wasn't ready to move on yet. "But I'm flattered," she said. "What exactly would you want me for?"

He made small circles with his espresso cup on the white tablecloth. "We're not interested in John's diagnostic work, frankly. Besides, it's all on public record. What we're interested in is his personal side project, the research he called AAD, alternate-area development. It could be a great help to us."

This time Susan was surprised. John's work in AAD had been considered so offbeat that it was virtually unknown to most of the medical community. Medical journals awaited "solid scientific evidence," and that evidence was still lacking, largely because of John's very limited funds.

It was well-known that areas around a damaged part of the brain sometimes took over the particular function of the injured tissue. "Helping out," John had called the complicated compensatory process. He believed certain areas could also be taught to respecialize in something not their normal function even when there was no damage. Make a motor-reflex area, for example, act instead to command language.

The key lay in deep electrode stimulation of designated brain areas and, using neurometrics, the subsequent computer analysis of the results. If success were ever achieved, John believed the capacity of the human race to think could be doubled, something he said would change the whole course of history. "For once," he would insist, "our minds might be in charge of our ridiculous emotions and leftover animal instincts."

Michael said, "Let me explain why, Susan. We are also into increased brain function, but with a different approach. Combining John's work with ours would accelerate our program incredibly, and we have a lot of pressure on us right now to do so."

"What exactly is your program?"

"I'm not free to give you a completely candid explanation," he replied. "Much of what we're doing has been classified by the government. But I can say this: we've developed a technique we call neurological blockage. It isolates all cerebral function from the body and relieves the brain of all reaction to such bodily problems as action and reflex, heat, cold, sex, hunger, et cetera. The brain can then concentrate on the purely abstract. Thinking, in other words."

"That certainly is different from John's theory," Susan protested. "It sounds almost like enforced quadriplegia."

"Quadriplegia, in a way, yes. But not enforced. Our subjects are all volunteers. We call them ECs— experimental cerebrals. The results we've had are remarkable."

"Like what?"

"In some cases we've upped actual brain use from the norm of around five to ten percent of its potential to nearly fifteen. With alternate-area development, we think we could add another ten percent, perhaps even more."

It staggered Susan. Michael had succeeded in attaining half John's goal already. Add John's system, and perhaps brain use could be increased to over three times its present level. The implications were enormous, perhaps as much so as in harnessing the atom. Such a quantum leap in man's ability to think could mean social and economic utopia instead of Armageddon. She began to understand some of the reasoning behind Borg-Harrison's insistence on secrecy.

She couldn't hide her excitement. "What you say is incredible, Michael." Then she came down to earth and shook her head. "But John's work was still mostly theory. There's a lot more to be done before it can be made practical."

He shrugged. "Whatever it takes, it takes. Your coming with us would make things a lot easier. Nobody understands John's work the way you do. But whether you do or not, I intend to see it become reality."

There was an intensity in him Susan had seen before only in John. How much alike they were, she thought, so brilliant and dedicated, both of them. And yet so very different. John all arms and legs, no one of his facial features quite matching the others, his manner often eccentric; Michael so handsome and charmingly urbane and fun to be with. How different was the inner Michael, the man she didn't know, from the vulnerable inner John who hid behind that cynical and often bristly exterior?

Driving home, she mulled unanswered questions about Michael's work. "Michael, who exactly are your volunteers?"

"They're people who would have died otherwise."

"Otherwise meaning the neurological blockage you spoke of?"

"Most of them, yes."

"It's a permanent thing, then?"

"In a way, yes."

There was something in his answer which was vaguely evasive. She started to ask more and then thought: To hell with it. She didn't want to talk about anything anymore which would make her think of work and John because she didn't want to think that John's work was the only reason Michael had asked her to dinner.

The darkness of the car, his presence, the soft-night glow of the dashboard gave her a wonderful feeling of isolation. She felt immune to the outside world, to the city around her, to any of the occasional pedestrians she saw, flitting shadows on pale-lit empty streets, for it was late now. For a brief time she had escaped loneliness. Too soon, the evening would end.

They swept up Constitution Avenue past the Capitol and minutes later pulled up before the house on Sixth Street.

Michael took her hand and thanked her for a lovely evening. "We'll do it again. Give some thought to my offer. No rush. You must have a lot of cleaning up to do anyway."

"I will consider it. I promise."

She stood in the doorway until his car's taillights disappeared and silence flowed in behind the sound of its motor. His job offer intrigued her. She was hardly John, but it would be wonderful to try to make his AAD theory work out. She could at least summarize and brief Michael on what had already been done so he could carry on from there.

In the spring, she decided, she'd run out to the Borg-Harrison lab, see what it was like, and make up her mind.

5

Admiral Walter Burnleigh smelled full-scale revolt. The oak-paneled boardroom, his twelve board members waiting silently the length of the long table for him to speak, was heavy with it. Even the expressionless faces of his several predecessors, preserved for posterity in expensive oil paintings, seemed accusatory.

As chairman, he'd had ample time during the last few months to dwell on the reasons for the trouble and prepare to deal with it. Five years ago he'd pressured the board to go outside the normal scope of Borg-Harrison's socioeconomic and military research, on which the foundation had built its prestigious reputation, and allocate twelve million dollars for a special brain-research program. Success in the research, he'd promised, might well offer America unchallenged hegemony in world affairs.

But time was running out. Due to be completed about now, the program needed at least another year to produce concrete results, and according to the figures provided today for each member in a gold-embossed folder, it had to date, due to spiraling inflation, cost thirty-eight million. Although the overall annual Borg-Harrison Foundation budget amounted to twenty times that amount, the figure for research at the laboratory the foundation leased from the National Institutes of Health at Bethesda exceeded that of any other program except for weapons testing and analysis of Russian satellite operations.

Borg-Harrison was no exception to the nation's economic problems, and on the printed page, the figures stood out like an offending sore.

With clear appreciation for his past leadership as well as his influence at the White House, his board, Burnleigh knew, would let him defend the huge cost overrun. After all, hadn't they also accepted the confining secrecy he'd imposed on the research? None of the twelve at the table had a clear understanding of anything the project involved except its goals. And they would allow themselves to be led once more by him.

Except for one thing. For all their intelligence, like many boards they were sheep. In part, he had only himself to blame for it. He had fashioned them that way. And if they could be led by him, so could they follow someone else. One voice among them, at this moment stronger than his, perhaps one who had already laid the groundwork at lunch, on the telephone or on the golf course, could lead them in the opposite direction.

He was pretty certain one was prepared to do just that, was even certain who among them it was. What he had to do was pull the man out and render him ineffective.

He stalled a last moment, adjusting his rimless glasses. Years before, he had hurt his eyes during thermonuclear testing at Eniwetok Atoll and the glasses were tinted. He found that an advantage. It made it difficult for others to read possibly betraying expressions.

He took in the gray and balding heads and lined faces looking back at him. They represented a broad spectrum of the nation's industry and commerce. Trans United Airlines; Universal Dynamics and Aero-Space; the giant brokerage house of Connors, Rosenstein, and Saul; Texas and Southwestern Petro-Chemical; Continental Micro Communications; others. Many contributed to the foundation, among whose clients were the Pentagon, the Department of State, the National Security Council.

He took a silent breath and said, "The figure before us is indeed unsettling and I understand your concern, although I assure you our research is finally very close to a major breakthrough."

He paused to focus on one particular board member, a dry emotionless man in his mid-sixties whose cold eyes were dark-circled and whose pale bony hands had a quality of mercilessness. He was president of the Union Credit and Commercial Trust Company, a holding corporation with a majority interest in a dozen leading banks which in turn had a vested share in most of the nation's industry.

Burnleigh put on a smile he didn't feel and went on. "I believe, however, that we are in much the same position as many of our leading banks with respect to their loans to emerging nations. When their debtors cannot meet their obligations, the banks more often than not have confidence in their reasons for making the loans in the first place and bear with them."

It bordered on naive. He had made it so deliberately, certain the banker would not be able to resist correcting him.

He was right.

The man spoke up, voice tinged with condescension and a confidence of victory he wasn't able to hide. "Mr. Chairman, I regret I have a certain problem with your analogy. Creditor banks are sometimes willing to adjust their loans, but only if they are able to evaluate accurately the economic future of their debtors. I see no parallel at all between that and this board being kept continuously in the dark about how our money is being spent. I believe we are all tired of vague claims about doubling the ability of the human brain to think and equating that possibility with the discovery of how to harness the atom. I move to vote now on the continuance of the research."

He was seconded.

Burnleigh smiled thinly. He'd flushed out the right man. Only his motivation hadn't been revealed. But he knew it well. His adversary's reasons were entirely selfish. The program's success would seriously injure his own personal ambitions to capture for himself the Borg-Harrison chairmanship with all the indirect political power that went with it.

Burnleigh nodded. "Very well. We'll put it to a vote. Before we do, however, the chair has a final statement to make."

Down the board table, for a fleeting instant, the bank president's eyes lit with triumph. Burnleigh knew just what the bastard was thinking. He was thinking he'd forced the chair into a position where it would try to sway the board's vote with an offer to resign. That was true. What he didn't know was that his move would backfire.

Burnleigh silently thanked his stars for the three years he'd spent as director of the CIA and for the firm loyalties he'd built in that organization.

And began guilelessly. "I would like, first of all, to clear up something I find deeply disturbing—and I am afraid I must again mention banking, although this time I do not believe it will be in vain." He favored the banker with another smile and went on to the board members. "Only recently this was revealed to me through connections I maintain with the CIA. While conducting a covert activity in an undeveloped African nation which involved many millions of dollars and the use of a private American bank to distribute them, it was discovered that an officer of that bank was using his position of trust to funnel some of those funds into financial areas beneficial to himself and counterproductive to the interests and aims of the United States of America."

He let it sink in, then said, "Is it possible that this

board thinks that I, as chairman, am doing the same with funds you have allocated to brain research? In view of the vital importance of the work, it's the only valid reason I can think of for your wanting to stop it."

He got the reaction he wanted. The bank president blanched visibly. The board members looked distressed.

"If so," he said, "I would like to offer my resignation to the board at once."

Five minutes later, he got the vote he wanted, approval for eighteen months' continuance of the program and for an additional four million dollars. In view of a potential scandal involving a chairman so close to the White House, the board quickly followed the surprise approving vote cast by the president of the all-powerful Union Credit and Commercial Trust Company.

Seeing the cold rage in the eyes of the man above the set smile of his narrow mouth, Burnleigh knew he'd made a mortal enemy. If the banker covered his tracks in Africa as quickly as Burnleigh thought he would, he'd have no further trump card with which to hold him in check at some future date.

A half-hour later he was back in his own luxurious office one flight above the boardroom. It was already six o'clock. The meeting had been unduly long. And tense. He sank wearily into the high-backed leather chair behind his memento-cluttered desk, ordered a much-needed Scotch, and told his secretary as she hurried to get it to put in a call to Dr. Burgess at the laboratory.

"Either Michael or Dr. Katherine Blair," he said.

While he waited for her to do so, he reflected briefly on those laws that governed the application of pressure at the top. In any organization, as the pressure was passed down it usually got worse. He was fond of Michael personally and believed in him and his work. Totally, God only knew, and to the extent of thirty-eight million dollars plus today's additional four, along with his own reputation. But although he and his staff were all dead tired, Michael was going to have to bear down hard now. Or else.

In this world, Walter Burnleigh reflected, every man had ultimately to look out for his own skin.

6

The winter proved long, spring exceptionally short. Summer, when it finally came, was welcomed with relief by everyone as far as the Carolinas.

On an early June Sunday, the sun over Oxford harbor on Maryland's eastern shore was burning hot and the temperature was a surprising and sultry eighty-seven. Al Luczynski, wearing an undersized bikini completely at odds with his round bearded face and big bearish body, stretched out on the worn scrubbed deck of the old schooner *Windigo* and soaked up the soothing rays. Last night, the bikini had caused such laughter from Katherine Blair that in a moment of beery defiance he'd stripped it off and swum without it. The others had followed suit, the dark water around each alight with bubbling phosphorus.

Katherine's laughter had seemed innocent enough, although with Katherine you never quite knew. There was always a personal edge to her cracks about anesthesiologists not really being real doctors and he couldn't ever forget the way she'd also laughed the night several years ago now when Michael was away and he'd drunk too much and made passes at her. He could still hear her. She'd laughed right in his face, not because of Michael but because she found him ridiculous. And he always had the feeling she still did.

He'd soon gotten over hurt feelings and anger, however, and with his old trick of mimicking voices, he'd added to the fun by confusing everyone in the darkness as to whom they were swimming next to. It had been a wonderful evening.

The *Windigo* belonged to Michael. Perhaps because he spent so much time in the high-tech atmosphere of an operating room, he preferred the archaic rigging and cavernous belowdecks of the old wooden boat to the artificial fanciness of a more modern yacht. This morning they had ghosted down the Chesapeake before the lightest of winds to have lunch and another swim in a secluded estuary.

It was noon, the water glassy calm. Occasionally the dying wake of some other boat would lap the schooner's hull and the *Windigo* would rock gently, causing the clear reflection of her two stubby masts and loosely furled graying sails to ripple in the silvery surface. A gull cried as it wheeled by; ashore, distant voices and the bark of a dog were muffled by heat.

From the galley below, Luczynski could hear Katherine and Toni Soong, Michael's assistant, getting lunch. Michael, stretched out in shorts under a canvas awning, had fallen asleep reading medical periodicals.

They'd all come down from Washington yesterday afternoon, himself and Toni Soong grateful for Michael's spontaneous invitation. It had been a harrowing week. They lost two ECs, one to surgery and the other to the psychosis which had already devastated several other volunteers during the winter. Michael especially had been jumpy and irritable, snapping at doctors and nurses alike, but today he seemed better. Probably that was Katherine's doing. When everyone had finally drifted off to bed, the sound of their lovemaking had come between their cabin and his, and Luczynski had buried his head under his pillow and tried not to visualize them.

Now, getting his mind off them again, the anesthesiologist rolled over to take the sun on his chest and to rub Bain de Soleil into the hair of his stomach. He'd thought once of trying to get some sort of relationship going between himself and Toni Soong. He'd always found her Asiatic good looks attractive, and last night, swimming naked, she'd seemed especially desirable. The sight of her high pointed breasts, the triangle of her thick pubic hair so dark against the moonlit paleness of her slim body and her musky rich female smell when she stood close, had made him want her badly. He'd had the feeling he could really make it with her if she'd given him half a chance. But Toni was either too involved with surgery to be sexual or had a secret case on Michael, he was never certain which. She had never given him the slightest encouragement, no matter what he hinted.

Katherine interrupted his thoughts. She came up from the galley carrying four fresh-boiled lobsters. She was wearing linen shorts and an expensive cotton beach blouse and looked more like a *Vogue* model than a neuropsychiatric shrink who dispensed the latest in chemistry to sick minds. Sometimes he wondered how much of Katherine's success in medicine was due to ability and how much to female wiles.

Then he forgot her a moment because Toni, like himself in just a bikini, came up with a tray bearing a huge salad, cheeses and fruit, and needed help.

Michael was shaken awake. Yawning, he opened their first bottle of luncheon wine and they all sat down to attack the lobsters at a table under the main deck's canvas awning.

After lunch, Toni caught Luczynski's eye and said she'd like to go for a row in the dinghy. "Maybe up the estuary a ways," she suggested, her dark eyes bland. "See if we can find some shells."

He was sensible enough to decide her invitation was just to let Michael and Katherine have a chance to be alone. As they pulled away from the schooner, she confirmed the thought. "They see us all week, Al, and in spite of asking us down, I just figured they might like to be alone for half an hour or so."

Luczynski resignedly leaned into the oars.

Katherine watched them go. "That was tactful of Toni."

"I thought maybe she'd finally decided to surrender." Michael absently threw a lobster claw at a passing gull, which wheeled up on one wing and caught it deftly.

Katherine laughed. "No chance," she said. "If for no other reason than that ridiculous bikini he insists on wearing." She saw Michael wasn't really listening and guessed why. They had a hard-and-fast rule to leave the lab behind on weekends, and he was thinking about work.

"Michael, you're cheating, aren't you?"

"Guilty. Sorry." He gave her a sheepish smile.

She sat next to him where he was lying on a sun mat. "Well, what was it?"

"The usual. How to get Burnleigh off our ass."

Katherine forced a smile. "Burnleigh's bark is worse than his bite."

"This time I don't think so. Last fall he gave us eighteen months and now that means only a year." He gestured helplessly. "The more we have to load too much work on the ECs, the more we get into trouble. The goddamn pressure is counterproductive."

Katherine said quickly, "Look, Michael, cut it out. We're going to make it. You know it, I know it. And with what we've already learned about Flemming's AAD, we're going to make it beyond our wildest dreams. When do we hear from McCullough?"

Michael's tone was evasive. "I'm not sure. I'm taking her to dinner tomorrow."

Katherine couldn't hide instant irritation. "Dinner? Why? For God's sake, what's the big deal? Why can't you just ask her, yes or no? Michael, it's important. Jesus, she's had since last December to decide."

He didn't answer directly. He frowned and said, "Katherine, some people just can't be rushed, you know that."

Katherine choked off a retort. They needed Susan McCullough. Badly. But Katherine was uneasy about her, always had been, and not just because of the security problem Susan might create. When they'd checked her out recently, they'd come across a pop-magazine article on brain research published the year before. A photograph showed Susan to be an almost seductively beautiful young woman. In a rangy, Midwestern way, of course. But Katherine suspected Michael's evasiveness stemmed from an interest in Susan McCullough that might just be a little more than purely professional. In her darkest thoughts it followed that if Michael actually had designs on Susan he might as well be having an affair with her already. Because Michael always got what he wanted, and always had. Katherine was suddenly struck by the irony. Here she was accusing him of cheating by thinking shop. It could be a good deal more serious.

She forced another smile. "Well, be as persuasive as you can."

He didn't answer. He'd closed his eyes to the sun, shutting her out, too.

Katherine poured herself some wine and thought: You're being silly, don't make something of nothing. Let him be the one to do that. Her irritation began to ebb, the dark wave of hostility, too. She thought of the trouble the research program was in and of herself and Michael.

Watching him drift off to sleep, she also thought of how they'd met. It seemed only just yesterday, the memory was still that vivid; the southwestern hospital where she'd interned; the blood-covered operating table, and under the white glare of operating lights, the dying patient, a wetback who had been half torn to pieces in a rail accident. She had been in awe of Michael's genius that saved a life almost all other surgeons would have lost; his smiling patience with her because she was fresh out of medical school and terrified.

And later, when she'd finished her internship, his scorn because she'd gone off to do psychiatry. "You've decided to be a shrink for only one reason, Katherine. Because your father is one. Why can't you just accept his being rich and famous and do your own thing? Surgery, for example."

Finally, she remembered how he had ignored her all during her psychiatric training. That had hurt even more. But he'd taken her in when she was qualified and never criticized her again. For five years since then, she'd worked long and hard and relentlessly, all the time keeping up Michael's morale so his brilliance could be directed constructively. She'd taken upon herself all the endlessly consuming administrative tasks that kept the program running and every problem, no matter how small, that had arisen with Burnleigh. She'd pinned everything on success, her whole future, in fact, and she wasn't about to let anything or anyone ruin any of it at this late date.

She began to clear up lunch. They had to be careful not to count too much on miracle results with Flemming's AAD theory. Somehow they had to try to accomplish more with their own research. EC burnout was crippling them and the only way she could see to cope with it was by finding more volunteers to work with. As every day passed, however, it was becoming more and more difficult to do so.

All the time she thought, Katherine kept coming back to Susan. Not Susan, the woman. That was a problem she'd decided she could deal with, should it be necessary. It was Susan the professional researcher who was most on her mind. She'd thought a great deal about Susan's future work for them, and one thing stood out clearly, something that for the time being she planned to keep strictly to herself. Like it or not, once Susan joined the lab she could never be allowed to stop work or leave. No matter what. When she signed a contract to work for Borg-Harrison, it would be for life.

7

Far up the estuary, Al Luczynski had beached the dinghy and he and Toni were searching for shells on a little strip of reed-bordered sand which ended where a brook ran into the salt water. It was a lovely and isolated spot. Marsh birds had flown up when they arrived, and a redwing screamed from his swaying clutch on a cattail, his wings bright slashes of crimson.

Toni was worried. Except for getting slightly drunk last night, she hadn't left work behind when they'd all piled into Michael's Mercedes and fled Washington.

They were under too much pressure, and too much pressure in Toni's experience often meant that things broke down. If Borg-Harrison should ever decide to close the lab, she'd be out of work, and then what?

Al was crouched, studying a shell. She said suddenly, "Al, if this deal should fold, where would you plan to go?"

He stood up. "The lab fold?" He immediately was guarded.

Christ, she thought, we're even getting secretive with each other. "If they decide to give up EC research, stick to cats and monkeys and fish. Ordinary stuff."

"I don't know." He toyed nervously with the shell. "I like Washington. I'd probably stay around."

She said pointedly, "Do you think anyone would have you?"

This time he looked at her sharply. "What the hell do you mean by that?"

"I mean," she answered carefully, "employ you after what you've been doing."

He stared, then turned away, avoiding her eyes.

"Well, do you?" she insisted.

"Why wouldn't they?"

"I didn't say they wouldn't," she went on, "I meant they might not because what we're doing might just shock the hell out of them. It might seriously disturb a lot of people. Not just doctors."

"Oh, come on, Toni, aren't you exaggerating a little? Anyway, how would they ever find out?"

"Well, if they didn't, then what would you say you'd been doing for the last five years? Driving a taxi? You know perfectly well that the moment the lab closed, someone would talk. And you know medicine. It would be everywhere in a week. Look, Al, we forget sometimes what the program's all about. Especially me, I guess, involved in the actual surgery with Michael. A lot of people might find us immoral, some might even see us as unethical. We tend to lose sight of that. We're so hopelessly involved with Michael's need to succeed, we could be guilty of forgetting what being a doctor really means. Sometimes I wake up nights and can't get back to sleep. Don't you ever?"

She guessed he did, the way he continued to examine his shell. But he didn't want to admit it because he didn't want to face it. Some people found certain things better hidden, even from themselves.

She knew she was right when he hedged. "Anesthesia is a little different from surgery, Toni. I don't have quite the same responsibility you do. It doesn't really make a damn bit of difference to me whom I keep under, or why, as long as they don't feel anything."

"What about Claire?"

His head snapped up, he went white, and Toni wished she hadn't asked. He'd been hopelessly infatuated with the nurse. When she'd nearly died from a ruptured spleen, Michael said she'd volunteered to become an experimental cerebral. Something had gone wrong during the operation, however, and she'd died anyway. Al had cried and cursed Michael and Katherine and claimed Claire never would have volunteered to be any kind of a guinea pig, that they had only taken her because before she became ill she'd had a row with Katherine and announced she was quitting. He'd accused Katherine of murder and asked who was safe at the lab if they took one of their own. He'd gotten terribly drunk for days. Michael advised everyone to be patient, and although Katherine had said Al was

59

neurotic and potentially dangerous, had kept him on. Two weeks later, Al was back to his old cheerful self, mimicking everyone's voice and eyeing any new nurse around. He had never mentioned Claire again.

"What about Claire?" she heard him demand. His voice was thin and his eyes like stone. Obviously he'd never forgotten Claire for one moment.

"I hate the bitch," he said. "I always will. It was her idea."

"Who?"

"Who the hell do you think? Katherine. I'd like to see her like Claire."

"Al, I'm sorry. Honestly."

She touched his shoulder affectionately and turned to glance at the sky. They'd been there awhile and the sun was visibly lower than when they'd left the boat. It was probably time to go back. A flight of crows, ragged black splashes against the hot blue-white of the sky, crossed the estuary a little farther up, calling raucously. And a fish splashed in the dead-calm water.

She hoped Al didn't really mean what he'd said about Katherine.

Someone who seemed so good-natured and secretly harbored that sort of anger was in trouble. Rumor among the nurses had it that Al was also impotent, that sex was all in his imagination. That was disturbing too. A guy who couldn't get it up often couldn't face it and would blame his problem on the woman or unconsciously resent all females everywhere.

Toni juggled the shells she'd collected. They would look nice in a shallow basket on the cocktail table in her Georgetown apartment. She thought about the place, its high-ceilinged spacious rooms, the tree-lined street outside with its immaculate private residences. She'd spent a lot of money and time making it perfect; expensive modern furniture, expensive modern paintings. It was almost unthinkable that she might have to give it up because she'd find herself out of a top-paying job and couldn't afford it any longer.

She turned toward the dinghy, which had begun to rock slightly with the slowly rising tide.

"I guess we'd better go," she said, "before that thing floats away."

"Whatever you want."

He sounded less truculent. She started back, leading, acutely conscious that his eyes were again probably on her hips and legs. All the time they'd been talking, she'd seen him trying to keep them from the thrust of her breasts against her bikini top and from the soft fullness of her pubic contour below.

She felt vaguely uncomfortable. The beach would be a great place for sex. Tanned naked bodies locked together on the yellow sands, their labored cries of ultimate ecstasy mingling with the scream of gulls and the call of wild birds and the sound of wavelets rustling shore pebbles. But not with Al. Last night when she'd stood close to him after their naked swim, she'd been very much aware of his wanting her. Something in her she'd recognized as rather cruel

61

had made her want to arouse him even further and see if the nurses were right or not before she said no. She was glad now she hadn't. Let someone else reject him. Besides, she'd had a hard enough time herself with her own reaction to Katherine. In the soft moonlight Katherine had seemed so different from the coolly remote woman she worked with every day. She'd slept restlessly afterward, vaguely jealous of Michael, whom she adored, wondering if there wasn't some safe way to strike a chord of response in Katherine and at the same time knowing she'd never dare try. The work they did was far too important to risk any embarrassment.

They reached the boat and pushed it into the water and got in. Luczynski rowed them back. He seemed to have recovered rapidly from his anger. Toni said a silent good-bye to the little beach. She always felt a sentimental attachment to lovely lonely places she knew she'd probably never see again.

She thought of Michael and Katherine again. Then she laughed at herself for being silly. Sun and sea and wine and nudity were a dangerous combination and could make you think ridiculous things you normally would never consider.

She began to think, instead, of the surgery she had to perform tomorrow. She was determined, for the rest of the evening, to think of nothing else.

8

The house on Sixth Street had too many memories. During the early spring Susan had moved to an apartment not far from the University Hospital Brain Research Laboratory. Michael picked her up there at six-thirty. He'd called earlier to say they'd drive out to the country for dinner.

Compared to the house, the apartment was tiny. There was only her bedroom, the kitchen, and a small living room. Since most of hers and John's furniture had belonged to his mother, she'd started fresh on her own. She had a simple platform bed and for a living-room couch some big puffy floor cushions in front of an old pine laundry table with sawed-off legs. Here and there she'd hung a few framed posters. It was all she could afford, but it already felt like home.

Through the parted curtains of her bedroom window she saw Michael's convertible pull up to the curb on the quiet street three floors below.

Double-locking the front door, she went downstairs, happy about the forthcoming evening. She hadn't seen Michael for more than three weeks. Tonight, the Susan he was taking to dinner was a whole new person. One morning, getting up, she'd decided she had to end her widowhood and once more be the independent woman she'd been for so long before John. She couldn't mourn him forever—she'd destroy herself—and she knew he'd be the first to agree. She could almost hear him sometimes urging her to stop mooning about and get on with life. He had been like that.

Something happened then. A weight lifted. She felt free and Michael began to appear in her thoughts, not just as a helpful friend and possible boss but as a very attractive and desirable man.

Coming home this evening, she'd suddenly thought: To hell with all the formality. You weren't supposed to mix business with pleasure, but so what! She shed her office clothes, showered, did her hair and nails, and put on a light summer dress with a daringly open back and a low-cut neckline. She spent an additional twenty minutes on her makeup and then was free with her favorite perfume. It had been a very long time since she'd taken this kind of trouble with herself, she realized. John had always seemed to prefer the blue-jeaned outdoor look, the Susan who was still back on the prairies and half tomboy, playing football with the boys in the schoolyard.

Downstairs, where Michael was waiting behind the wheel of his car, she suffered a brief stab of doubt. Jesus, McCullough, she thought, he'll think you have designs. Then she laughed at herself and slid into the front seat beside him. So what if he did? Maybe that wasn't such a bad thing.

"Hi."

"You look wonderful."

"I feel wonderful. Where are we going?"

"The Old Teamster."

She remembered it, a country restaurant in Virginia about forty-five minutes away.

Michael knew Washington well and managed to avoid most of the last of rush-hour traffic except for the Key Bridge crossing the Potomac out of Georgetown. The suburbs to the west gave way to a belt of woods and then to soft rolling fields and farms. The sun was setting when the Blue Ridge Mountains finally came in sight.

The early-summer evening was soft. Susan leaned her head back against the seat and luxuriated in the rich fresh smell of the countryside. "It's so damn good to get out of the city."

"Do you sail?"

"No, I'm from the Midwest, remember? But I'm willing."

"I have an old boat across from Annapolis. Plan a weekend going down the Chesapeake sometime."

"I'd love to."

They never made it to the Old Teamster. At the next small town there was a country fair with a 4-H Club livestock show, a Ferris wheel and other rides, a shooting gallery, and a score of game booths. Something quickened in Susan. Every year, her father and mother had taken her to the country fair down south near Winner.

"Oh, Michael, let's stop."

"I'm game."

He pulled into the huge field that served as a parking lot and for the next two hours they filled up on junk food and soda and took all the rides from the whip to the sky rocket. They went to the fun house, laughed at their grotesquely fat and thin images in the curved mirrors. They pitched pennies and shot archaic .22s at rows of shot-worn wooden ducks and rabbits, and Susan won a ridiculous plastic doll as large as the wide-eyed little girl she immediately gave it to.

In a blood-red tent covered with yellow half-moons, stars, and hex signs, a white-haired Gypsy woman told their fortunes from tarot cards and their palms.

"You will have two lovers," she told Susan. "One for his body, the other only for his mind." To Michael she said, "And you are two people, one disguised by the other. A jealous woman could ruin you both."

When they laughed, she grew furious and threatened to put a curse on them.

They left and watched a trotting race and afterward went and looked at blue-ribbon sheep and poultry and cattle.

A two-week-old Jersey calf sucked on Susan's fingers, its tongue wet-raspy and its breath sweet. She felt a kind of nostalgia she hadn't felt for years. "Sometimes I wonder," she said, "if what we all do is real—labs, computers. This little guy somehow

66

makes it seem crazy." She scratched the calf behind his ears and said, "My father always wanted to have a dairy farm. He hated chickens. But he never could raise enough money."

Inexplicably, she began to cry. "I'm sorry, Michael. I guess we'd better go."

He took her back to the car and they headed for Washington. They were quiet and hardly spoke. Susan was embarrassed. She felt she'd ruined the evening. From time to time she glanced sideways at him. Any woman would have to feel flattered to be out with Michael. More than ever, she was conscious of his strong sexuality. She'd grown unaccustomed to that side of men. John had been a thinker and a dreamer. In her life with him the excitement had been more in the world of the mind they shared so totally. John's brilliance and eccentric charm had somehow made up for an infrequent physical passion.

She said suddenly, "I turned out to be a great date, didn't I?"

"No problem."

He touched the back of her head and rested his hand on her shoulder. It was electric; she could feel him through her whole body.

They came into Washington and again she felt the wonderful sense of isolation she'd felt the first time he'd driven her home, with the soft glow of the car's instruments once more making a unique world just for them. She was unaware of anything else until they stopped. They were on a strange street in front of a strange building.

"My place," he said. "We'll have a drink."

Susan's heart leapt. The car's clock said eleven. "Don't you have to operate tomorrow?"

"I can do it with my eyes shut."

He got out of the car abruptly and headed for a front door. Susan followed. This means bed, she thought. Do I want this? With Michael?

Even as she thought it, she knew she did. Had wanted it for weeks, ever since she'd stopped feeling like a widow, and had known it was inevitable, too. When he opened the door and showed her in, his hand warm against the bareness of her back, she felt herself shaking with anticipation.

His apartment on the top floor of the five-story building was a very large studio with skylights and big sliding glass doors that opened onto a gardened terrace where a wrought-iron stair wound up to another garden on the roof. He poured some ice-cold white wine and they took it outside to sit on a settee. Susan tucked her legs up under her. The open back of her dress and its deep neckline suddenly made her feel completely naked.

He said softly, "You've been driving me nuts for weeks. You must know that."

She made a halfhearted attempt to retreat.

"Michael, we shouldn't be doing this."

"Is it John?"

"No. It's not John." But was it? Was she frightened she'd suddenly think of him in the middle of it and go to pieces? She'd thought not. Now, at the last moment, she wasn't sure.

"You were going to say work, maybe?"

She hedged. And couldn't help flirting slightly. "Not really. I was thinking about her."

He looked surprised. "Who?"

"Whoever. There's got to be someone in your life. I won't believe you if you say there isn't."

He shrugged. "For the occasional thing, of course."

"At least you're honest. Is she nice?"

"Yes. We're good friends."

"But you're not in love?"

"No."

"Does she love you?"

"I don't know. She's never said so. I hope not."

"If it's just for sex, then, why is there just one person?"

He smiled. "I'm too busy to be so complicated. And I don't have a pasha complex."

Susan studied him, then put down her drink. Her heart raced and her mouth was dry. She could hardly hear her own voice. She said, "Want to know something?"

"What?"

"To hell with her."

He kissed her then, very gently at first, then with more passion. He took her by the hand to his wide low bed and began to undress her. She felt herself floating and helpless. When he undressed himself and then held her close and she felt his long hardness against her abdomen, a rushing weakness swept through her, and when he began to kiss her neck and breasts, she let her own hands explore, fingers tracing his thighs and the flat planes of his stomach, enjoying the exquisite and instant response in herself that touching him brought her. There was nearly pain now in her urgent need to have him.

She knew he was making her wait. His mouth explored downward. She thrust up against him, wanting him to stop, wanting him not to at the same time. She held his head between her legs, running her fingers through his thick hair. The warm searching heat of his mouth obliterated everything except her need for release.

It came suddenly and in waves. She let herself go. And then again, and again, aware only of the sensations she felt, not where she was or what she was doing. And vaguely she heard her own voice cry out from somewhere.

What he made her feel kept on and on until its intensity was knife-edged. But just when she couldn't stand any more, he seemed to know and joined her, his first long thrust deep and strong and then the slow driving rhythm he began seeming to fill her entire body with him, his arms beneath her shoulders holding her tight up against him, his buttocks like marble.

The rhythm accelerated. His smell was musk and animal, she felt the hardness of his muscles against her breasts, his breath began to labor. She let herself go again, thrusting back. And then was aware of nothing except his cries, muffled in her neck and hair, the rigid shuddering of his entire body. And the bursting heat she felt course through her when he came. She was caught up in a violence which carried her up and up and into oblivion.

Afterward there was the long lazy delicious sensation of returning to self; lassitude and drifting in a half-dream.

She became aware of him again, still in her, gently kissing her mouth.

"Hi."

"I can't believe what you made me feel."

Her arms tightened around him. She didn't want him ever to leave her. The weight of his body when he relaxed was a delicious cover of warmth and protection, a blanket securing everything she'd felt, letting nothing of what they'd shared escape.

"Do you want a drink?"

"Yes, please."

Without withdrawing, he helped her half-sit, held her wineglass to her lips. She drank, kissed his shoulder and chest, and lay down again, pulling him onto her.

"Where did we go?"

"Don't know. I got lost somewhere."

"So did I."

She kissed his face and opened her mouth to his.

It was a very gentle kiss, his tongue soft and quiet against hers.

She felt a faint stab of pleasure. Then another. And miraculously, he started to grow within her again. His kiss became harder, his mouth more insistent. His body moved against hers. She felt herself respond.

A brief vision of John swam somewhere behind her eyes, then went out like a light. This wasn't John and never had been. This was Michael.

Her arms went tight around his back once more.

This time there was a whole new sensation, a hot abandoned carnality. He seemed enormous in her, everything. His body became hers, and hers his, fiercely familiar now, violent in need and possessiveness, the splayed female, the plunging male.

Nothing in the world was of any importance except their two bodies merged into one.

Much later, just before they slept, Susan suddenly thought of the old Gypsy woman at the country fair. "You'll have two lovers," she'd said. "One for his body, the other only for his mind."

How utterly ridiculous, Susan thought.

9

Three mornings later, Susan drove out to the brain-research laboratory Borg-Harrison leased from the National Institutes of Health.

The visit was a formality. She knew she would accept Michael's job offer. How could she do otherwise? She'd come to an end of John's work, and although the security she felt at the old lab was tempting, there was no particular challenge in what they wanted her to do. It was the perfect time to move on.

Besides, there was Michael himself. She'd never experienced any man like him. Her memory of their second night together and the morning that followed was still vivid. She had awakened to see him standing in the bedroom doorway with coffee, naked except for a towel slung casually over one shoulder, his body lean and muscular and beautiful, and the thought that she might ever have to give him up seemed impossible.

At Ward Circle, opposite the gray-stone building and oak trees of American University, she turned onto Nebraska with its quiet suburban side streets and homes and then took Wisconsin out of the District and into Maryland.

Traffic thinned. She was going against the commuter rush and soon found herself at the National Institutes of Health. She drove through a brick-columned entrance and then down one of the many smooth blacktopped streets which wound among the lawns and shrubbery separating the individual institutes, clinics, and laboratories which made up the NIH's sprawling acreage.

She found the Borg-Harrison research lab at the end of a quiet tree-lined cul-de-sac. It was an isolated three-story brick building with its own parking lot.

She left her car and went in.

The lobby was modern with a fountain, plants, and indirect lighting and divided by a counter with a turnstile watched over by an unsmiling young female security guard who wore a holstered revolver. Arrogant, Susan thought.

"I have an appointment with Dr. Burgess. My name is McCullough. Susan McCullough." She made it very formal. She had decided that at all costs she had to keep her work relationship with Michael completely separate from personal feelings. No one must have even a hint of their intimacy.

The guard telephoned the information to someone and asked Susan to sign a form stating the purpose of her visit.

Susan complied. She'd expected security, but not so much. Almost immediately, however, a woman in her early thirties appeared. She wore a white medical coat and had titian hair held back in a French chignon. Susan thought her outstandingly attractive. A lapel ID card said she was Dr. Blair. She would be the associate Michael had mentioned.

Amber eyes took in Susan. She smiled warmly. "Susan? Hello. I'm Katherine Blair. Did you have any trouble finding us?"

Susan said she hadn't and heard that Michael was unexpectedly tied up in surgery but would be finished in just a few minutes.

Katherine unclipped her ID, inserted it into a slot in the turnstile, allowing Susan through. At the far end of the lobby she repeated the process at a door marked "Authorized Personnel Only." She offered Susan an apologetic smile. "Sorry for all the heavy security. Admiral Burnleigh, the foundation's chairman, is a little nuts on the subject."

Beyond the door was a long corridor. A second guard barred access to it. Susan signed her name again. She noticed a closed-circuit TV monitor which gave the guard a view of some other security post in an open lobby someplace.

"That's our surgical section on the third floor," Katherine explained. "Down here is just offices. The second floor houses our cafeteria, most of the research labs, and the computer mainframe. We have a Data General Eclipse MV 8000."

"All your own?"

"All our own." Katherine laughed. "Borg-Harrison

gave us a blank check when we opened this place, and we went wild."

She led the way down the corridor. It was carpeted, quiet. Doors gave onto a records room, a personnel department, various other offices. They reached one which led to a secretarial foyer and a desk where Susan was introduced to Gladys, an underweight middle-aged redhead who wore rhinestone harlequins dangling from a chain around her neck. Gladys, Katherine declared, was the person who actually ran the place.

Beyond Gladys were two other offices, both cheerful and sunny. In one Susan saw bookcases of medical texts and periodicals, photographs and prints of sailing boats. The desk was large, modern, and uncluttered.

"That's Michael in there," Katherine said. She led Susan into the second office, where there were window plants and attractive reproductions of various French impressionists. "And this is me. There's something I have to ask you to sign and then I'll introduce you to Henry Palmer. He's dying to meet you."

Michael had mentioned Dr. Palmer. He was a neurologist and neurophysiologist specializing in psychobiology. Before he'd recently joined Borg-Harrison he'd done some interesting and innovative work in neurometrics up at an important brain lab in New York. He was good but he wouldn't be John.

Katherine produced a printed form. "Once again, my apologies, but we've all had to sign this. It's because some of the work we do for the government is highly classified."

Susan read that the revelation by her of anything she heard or saw at the lab would be regarded as a breach of national security punishable under federal law. "Wow!" she said.

Katherine laughed. "I know. That's what we all said when we first read it."

Susan signed and they went back out to the corridor where Katherine called an elevator by using her ID card, then selected the second floor stop the same way.

"Every person's card is coded," she explained, "to give him access to wherever his security clearance allows him."

The elevator stopped. They got out and crossed a small lobby to Laboratory Research and Susan found herself in a neurophysiologist's paradise. There seemed to be every conceivable kind of equipment necessary for brain research, from a heavy, squat electroencephalogram console and a sound-proof-light-proof testing booth to the latest PETT, Positron Emission Tranaxial Tomograph scanner which photographed sections of the brain, both horizontally and vertically.

There was a battery of computers, including the latest in neurometric translators and one large terminal geared to three-dimensional studies of CAT scans using the Shelton Stereotactics technology. There was electrophysiology amplification equipment which could pick up the electrical activities of neurons in millivolts and translate it onto grid paper and there was Hewlett Packard biofeedback gear along with a special built-in thermal printer.

A small graying little man rose from the desk and came to meet her. "Hello, hello, Susan McCullough. This is so exciting for me. I'm Henry Palmer."

He had an air of a slightly fuzzy grandfather and Susan liked him at once. Within minutes, he had taken her on a tour of adjoining laboratories where white-smocked researchers were conducting optic brain studies on fish and monkeys. She was introduced to a half dozen grad students and chose to skip the "kennel" where they kept experimental rats and monkeys. Caged laboratory animals had always bothered her, no matter how necessary. She found the monkeys' inevitable insanity very upsetting.

"You'll work in the central lab with me if you want," Palmer declared. "Or we can put up a partition, so you can shut yourself away. I hardly pretend to have John Flemming's genius, but perhaps with your close personal knowledge of his studies and techniques, we can make a little sense together."

"He's awfully nice," Susan said to Katherine, when they'd gone on to the cafeteria, "and I simply can't believe the equipment you have." They had found a table and brought coffee to it before Michael suddenly appeared with two other people, both clearly doctors. One was a big, bearded man, the other an attractive young Asiatic woman. Michael was professionally formal. He apologized for being late and introduced the others. "Al Luczynski, our anesthesiologist—don't be put off by his looking like a bear.

Or by somebody else's voice coming from his mouth. He's actually harmless. And this is Toni Soong. Toni does most of our surgery while I kibitz."

Susan found them as friendly as Henry Palmer. When Katherine had to leave, "for, of all things, a doctor's appointment," she nodded at Al Luczynski. "I do hope you decide to join us, Susan, if for no other reason than to help keep this one in line."

Luczynski blushed above his beard, and to Susan's astonishment imitated Katherine perfectly. Everyone laughed. Susan watched Katherine go out. Once when Michael had first come in she'd seen an odd expression flit across Katherine's eyes. A kind of anxiety touched with a vague hostility. Why?

Downstairs in Michael's office she kept formality going. An important aspect of her job still remained obscure. "Michael, what about the volunteers? I'd like to talk to one or two."

He didn't answer immediately. Then he said, "I'm afraid you can't."

She was surprised. "Because I'm not here officially?"

"Even when you are." He smiled and held up a hand against her immediate protest. "I know it must seem ridiculous; you have to work with them. But it's their choice, I'm afraid. They want no contact with anyone except a few of the nurses and doctors on staff—myself, Soong, Katherine, Al Luczynski, and recently Palmer. For the time being, we'll have to place scalp electrodes where you tell us you want them, and of course the deep ones, which we'd have to do anyway."

It left Susan feeling uncomfortably stymied, but somehow she wasn't surprised in view of the vague answers he'd given to some questions she'd asked in the past. Obviously the security at Borg-Harrison consisted of more than guards.

He seemed to read her thoughts. He said abruptly, "Look, Susan, you think I'm not telling you all about our program. Well, you're right. There are aspects of it I can't go into with anyone until they've been with us for a while. Eventually, of course ... but at the beginning, no. That thing you signed—it wasn't just nonsense. We're dealing with some very sensitive research. Does that help?"

Oddly, it did. Isolation from the volunteers wouldn't make her work impossible, she thought, and he'd virtually said it wouldn't last forever.

She smiled and made it brisk. "Okay, Dr. Burgess, Dr. Palmer suggested a partition so I can close a door on myself. I'll also want a Data General terminal compatible with your Eclipse mainframe, and even if you think you have everything, you don't, so be prepared to install some special neurometric gear John came up with, and it won't be cheap. You have two weeks."

Michael rose from his desk. "I'll be equally brief," he said. He pulled her to her feet and kissed her hard and quickly. "And that's the last time that will happen here, Miss McCullough."

He opened his door. "Gladys, break out Coca-Cola or whatever obnoxious non-champagne we drink when we've just enrolled a new genius."

A half-hour later, when Michael saw her out to

her car, Susan had one last moment of weakness. Had she made her decision for the wrong reason, because of Michael and not because of the job itself? She hoped not. Once or twice as they went, their shoulders touched. It was familiar and exciting to her and she had to force herself to think only about the work ahead and to reassess in her mind the problems associated with it.

But alone, as she drove home she couldn't suppress her personal feelings any longer. Washington had never looked so glorious, and tomorrow night, when he'd come to pick her up for dinner, was several light-years away.

10

A week later, Katherine drove over to the Borg-Harrison Foundation's national headquarters situated just off Embassy Row on Massachusetts Avenue. Formerly an ambassadorial residence, it was approached by a driveway which curved from the tree-lined street through massive iron gates, then across a shaded lawn, broken here and there by tailored shrubbery and flowerbeds.

To Katherine, the imposing nature of the place always came as a slight surprise. Dealing all day with the lab's introverted world, she tended to lose sight of the foundation's many other activities: the think-tank advice it provided the government as well as private industry, its political and military evaluation of other nations, its research in biogenetics as well as in ecology and the environment, its pioneering studies into light, laser development, and ultrasound.

Admiral Burnleigh's office was on the second floor,

with French doors opening onto a balcony looking down over the driveway.

It was reached by a sweeping open stair that rose up from a marble front hall decorated with busts of former Presidents of the United States and American primitive paintings in gold-leaf frames.

Katherine found him not there. He'd been detained at a meeting at the White House. His secretary showed her into his office, brought her coffee and the *Washington Post*, and Katherine sat in a deep leather chair and waited.

She'd felt acutely anxious and had done everything she could think of to boost her confidence, including spending more time than usual on her appearance, her makeup, hair, and selecting what to wear.

The effect wasn't for Burnleigh, however. Burnleigh was not one to be swayed by feminine beauty or wiles. The effect was for herself. Where Burnleigh was concerned, she counted on a slightly different kind of leverage.

She'd laid the groundwork for it five years before when she'd first pressed Michael to let her work with him. She knew she'd have to be screened by Burnleigh himself at Borg-Harrison, since Michael spoke of him as taking a direct personal interest in the project. Without Michael's knowledge, she called Burnleigh cold and went to see him, making no attempt to hide her ambition for a greater role than that of staff psychiatrist on the research project. If she could eventually attain a position at headquarters which would place all future Borg-Harrison medical matters under her control, she would finally have reached the same stature as her father.

Faintly amused, he'd demanded to know what she considered her special qualifications and she'd told him with equal candor, "Sir, without meaning any disloyalty to Michael, he's a scientific and medical genius, not a businessman. You're spending millions at the lab and I should think it would be important to you to have someone there you can trust to let you know the way things actually are. Not the way someone might think they are or hope they are."

He'd studied her, mind and thoughts concealed behind steely eyes that revealed nothing, then had suddenly made his decision. He'd laughed, one of the rare times she'd ever heard him do so. Laughed and called her a born politician. "My man at the lab, my dear girl? Why not?" And had taken her out to an expensive lunch to seal an unspoken bargain in which each planned to use the other and be ungrudgingly used in return. They had never jeopardized the arrangement by going to bed, although there were times when Katherine knew they both wanted to. Burnleigh had achieved the kind of success she found very seductive.

Now, idly taking in the personality of the office, she tried to match it up with the man she knew.

There were the usual signed photos of various Presidents and foreign heads of state. There were shelves of law and naval books, prestigious periodicals, pictures of children and grandchildren, framed diplomas and honorary degrees. Eleanor Burnleigh,

Boston Brahmin to the core, stared from a silver photo frame with kindly eyes and the white hair of her sixty years.

None of it revealed more than other offices did about other equally high-ranking public servants. Except for a photograph of the admiral as a cadet at Annapolis that showed a slight young man in whose eyes, far older than his years, there was iron will. Katherine had often seen the same look in the Burnleigh she knew.

She had finished her second cup of coffee before he finally appeared, the same slight man of the photograph but gray now and his eyes framed by rimless tinted glasses.

"Sorry, my dear. The President's such a damn fool with all his good-old-days and 'right-stuff' Air Force stories. It makes some meetings take forever. There are times I wish the hell he'd never seen an airplane."

She accepted his kiss on her cheek and when he'd seated himself behind his massive desk, wasted no time. "I have this to present to you, Admiral. You won't like it but we must have what it describes immediately."

She took a single-page memorandum from her briefcase and watched while he studied it.

When he put it down, his face was without expression but he picked up a small gold pencil from its neatly appointed place by his desk blotter and began to roll it gently between thumb and forefinger. Long ago, Katherine had learned the idiosyncrasy was a barometer of his irritation.

He said, "Why?"

"Because," Katherine answered, "McCullough says she and Flemming always figured they could have accelerated his work a hundred percent if they'd been able to afford that sort of equipment. In view of the commitment we've made to Flemming's alternate-area development, I think we ought to give her anything she wants."

He continued to roll the pencil a moment before he spoke again. Then he said, "What did you make of McCullough, I mean now that she's finally on board and working?"

Katherine had expected the question and had prepared a carefully neutral answer. The uneasiness she felt at the interest in Susan that Michael hadn't been able to hide completely was none of Burnleigh's business. She said, "Professionally speaking, I find her well balanced enough. She seems to have no particular quirks except a sort of unawareness of self, perhaps. But that's often the case with grad students, usually because of preoccupation with their work."

"What about security?"

"So far, we've had no problem. And I don't think we will."

Burnleigh smiled thinly. "I hope you're right, Katherine, I hope you're right. How about where Dr. Palmer is concerned?"

"Palmer has serious money worries, which were solved for him when he joined us. He does what I ask, especially with anything involving McCullough."

Burnleigh glanced at the memo again. "If we give

her this equipment, how long is it going to take her to make it pay for itself?"

"That would depend on Flemming's theories and what help both she and Palmer might be in making them practical."

"Has she intimated anything?"

"She thought at least a year."

Burnleigh put his gold pencil down. He said, "I tried to make it clear to Michael recently that a year is all we have."

"He understood, sir, but when we launched the program we didn't count on unforeseen economic problems causing big budget overruns that in turn forced us to put pressure and hurry-up workloads on the ECs that they simply can't handle. They're cracking up left and right. Paranoia, schizophrenia, hysteria, you name it, we hardly bring one group to scratch and it's decimated. If this keeps up—and I can't see that it will do otherwise—we're not going to have any ECs left whom we can use for anything, let alone Flemming's AAD experiments. McCullough, as well as all this equipment she's asked for, will be a complete waste."

Burnleigh remained expressionless. His eyes behind their tinted lenses appeared as dark pinpoints. He said, "What are you doing about this insanity? Medically, I mean? Can't some of the new drugs help?"

"I'm already using the full range of all the anti-schizophrenic, antidepressant and tranquilizing psychopharmaceuticals that exist, from diazepam—that's plain old Valium—and impiramine to lithium. It's like trying to stop an avalanche."

"How many working at present?"

"ECs? Only five. We lost another last week."

"There's no way you can find a greater number of them?"

"Yes, sir. But you won't let us use it."

"Katherine, if I let you use the VA, we'd have that whole damned bureaucracy breathing down our necks night and day, and you know it, and that's the last thing we need. Have you considered prospecting outside the Washington area?"

"Of course, but we'd be getting into hospital records systems controlled by people we didn't know and couldn't control, a whole host of things Michael and I both felt would be pretty risky." She hesitated before adding, "There's another alternative I believe we already discussed once."

She waited. Burnleigh shot her a quick penetrating look, then ignoring her remark, handed her back the memorandum she'd given him. "Alright, you can go ahead with this. I just hope it isn't pouring good money after bad." He carefully aligned his pencil in its allocated place beside his blotter and rose. The meeting was over.

But at the door, he stopped abruptly. "Twice, not once. And unofficially. Twice before you came in here with specific requests concerning unorthodox procurement of two particular ECs. I told you both times you were on your own with that and be damned careful." He smiled faintly. "You seem to have managed successfully and if I know you, I suspect with more than just the two in question. But if you're again asking official approval, I still won't give it to you. I'll only repeat what I said then. Do what you must but remember, neither Borg-Harrison nor I will be or can be part of any possible repercussions. I hope I make myself clear."

"Yes, sir."

He saw her down to the front door, gallantly taking her arm as they descended the wide red-carpeted stairs to the spacious hall below and filling her in on news of his children and grandchildren.

The security guard stood at attention as he walked her out to her car. As she braked at the end of the driveway before entering Massachusetts Avenue just beyond the massive front gates, she looked back.

He was still standing on the front steps watching her. She knew it was his way of lending moral support for her doing what was now more necessary than ever, in spite of refusing to sanction it officially, and she was grateful, because the risks she was taking were great. She couldn't ask for more.

11

Few autopsy rooms are anything but cold and cheerless places. The one at the Borg-Harrison lab was no particular exception.

It was small and low-ceilinged, with intense overhead light but with the temperature maintained at a cool fifty-eight degrees Fahrenheit. There was a refrigeration unit sunk into one wall, containing a dozen lockers for those deceased who were awaiting postmortem investigation, and on several shelves of a tall cabinet, glass containers in which various specimens of brain matter were preserved. There was a stainless-steel table with drainage facilities and also the usual instrument cases and drawers for everything including electric saws and drills.

In an adjoining room, there was a Formica-topped bench supporting several high-powered microscopes including an elaborate electron microscope unit capable of a several-hundred-thousand-times magnification. And there were special files designed for glass slides where tissue, blood, or other matter was under current investigation.

It was late Saturday afternoon, nearly five-thirty. Few at the lab ever regarded the week as over on Friday and Toni Soong was no exception. She had been working for some time sectioning the left temporal of a female brain and cataloguing sections for future examination when she became aware of someone in the doorway watching her.

She looked up. It was Sara.

The nurse came in to stand close by the autopsy table. Toni tried not to be disturbed by her blond beauty and youthful figure, apparent in spite of her starched white uniform, or by imaginings of tonight, when, dressed like women and not in sexless medical uniforms, they would make dinner together at Toni's apartment with brandy and coffee and a whole blissful evening to follow. Henry Palmer had the Saturday night-Sunday morning duty. A few more minutes and she would be free until six A.M. Monday, when she had to prepare for an eight-o'clock operation.

She said matter-of-factly, "I'll be through shortly, and you're not really supposed to be here." And then kicked herself mentally when Sara looked instantly stricken.

"Sorry," Sara said. "I just wanted to tell you I might be a few minutes late this evening. I'll try not to be."

Toni's sense of guilt increased. Why did the girl have to be so insecure? She told her not to worry and watched her go out and then began to clean up. The phone rang.

"Autopsy. Dr. Soong."

It was Susan McCullough. "Toni, sorry to call so late, but would it be possible for you to stop down here a moment before you go home?"

"What's the problem, Susan?"

But she knew very well what the problem would be and hoped any irritation she felt wouldn't show. Even though she'd been there a month, Susan was still denied access to all experimental cerebrals, and the problem was electrodes.

Deep electrodes used to stimulate the brain were one thing. Often inserted far down into the brain's deepest interior, they were charged with several milliamperes of electricity, which influenced brain activity. Inserting them called for cutting windows in the skull and then delicate neurosurgery by herself or Michael.

Scalp electrodes, Susan's usual problem, were used to record and transmit brain waves onto the electroencephalogram and were quite a different matter. You simply stuck the electrodes right over the hair onto the scalp with a special adhesive which made them easy to get off. It was a job for any first-year grad student. To no avail she'd tried to persuade both Michael and Katherine to change Susan's security status and give her a card which would allow her access at least to the EC she was experimenting with.

She heard Susan say, "It's on the EC named Helen, Toni. I've charted out where I want the electrodes replaced or moved." Her voice had the awkward tone of one who realizes she's putting someone else out. "I'd ask Dr. Palmer, but he's got something going he can't leave just yet."

"Don't worry about it, Susan. I'll be right down."

Five minutes later, Toni entered the research lab on the floor below. Palmer was still at his desk, frantically working out a mathematical formula to be used in deep electrode analysis. On his specially converted computer, the electroencephalogram readings of his EC's brain waves appeared as numbers rather than as zigzagging green lines.

He smiled at Toni. "Sorry, Doctor, if I leave this now it's two days' work down the drain."

Toni nodded. She suspected old Palmer couldn't reconcile the restrictions on Susan with all the attention Michael was giving her.

She knocked on Susan's door and went directly into a small office that was jammed with computers and electronic devices and a desk piled with print-outs and data sheets. The room had taken on its cluttered appearance from the day Susan had moved in. Toni wondered how she could make any sense of it. Or of the incredibly complex computer programming and mathematics involved. Michael said she could, however, and was clearly excited by her progress. He had already instilled a sense of urgency in Susan, and she daily worked nearly twelve-hour stretches and sometimes longer.

Toni also wondered about Katherine's reaction. These days, Michael was more often found in Susan's office than in his own, edging out poor Al Luczynski, who'd developed a crush on Susan the moment he'd laid eyes on her. How jealous would Katherine be beneath her impeccable psychiatrist's exterior which nothing ever seemed to ruffle? Or would she be jealous at all? Remembering the unexpectedly different Katherine she'd seen on Michael's boat that early-summer night, Toni thought perhaps she might be. And if she were, God help everyone.

Susan gave her a grateful smile and showed her the scalp-electrodes chart, which by now had become all too familiar.

"I know it's Saturday and late and you must be almost on your way out, but before you go, if you could just change the frontals to these two positions, the four on the parietal replaced to here, here, here, and here. That's for a start. And could you possibly up the per-minute pulse on the left thalamus deep probe to, say, four? It's at two right now. And a tenth of a milliamp increase?"

Toni cursed inwardly. There'd be thirty minutes' work to do, perhaps more, before she could go. She wouldn't get home until after seven and would have to tear around like crazy tidying up and rushing out to the supermarket. Thank heaven Sara would be late too.

"I'll take care of it immediately," she said.

"Thanks, Toni."

Toni went to the door, stopped. "And listen," she said. "Whatever happened to women's lib? To hell with these guys. Knock it off for the weekend! Get some rest. Doctor's orders."

"I'll try." Susan's smile was wan.

When Toni had gone, she leaned her head back and closed her eyes for a moment. She felt beat. Toni was right: she ought to take it easy. But she couldn't stop work yet. Not until she'd finished today's testing. She'd canceled sailing with Michael to do so and might have to come in tomorrow, like it or not. She was getting exciting results with an AAD experiment in language memory. John had left considerable data on how to work it, and Palmer had come up with some fresh ideas almost equally good.

Then there was Michael himself. He seemed under tremendous pressure of some kind and clearly relieved at any progress she reported, although he still wouldn't relent on her seeing the EC she was working with, despite the fact that she kept telling him it would speed up her work considerably. Last weekend she'd gone sailing with him for the first time. It was after dark before they'd finally broken free from work and started for the boat. They'd gotten underway at once and ghosted down Chesapeake Bay under the lightest of night breezes. By the golden light of a full July moon they had anchored in a quiet cove and slept on deck. At breakfast, perhaps because the evening had been so perfect, she hadn't been able to resist talking about her work. Eventually she'd made one more plea to change her security status and give her an ID card which would allow her access to the third floor.

"It's uncanny, Michael. Helen's becoming real to me. As though I had actually met her and not just her neuron activity. She's middle-aged, brilliant, and warm. She rarely gets excited. Most extraordinary, her activity level is nearly forty percent higher than normal." Then she'd added, "Please let me meet her, Michael. All this secrecy is becoming counter-productive."

He'd rebuffed her, pleasantly but firmly. And she'd flared. "Oh, for God's sake! What the hell have you got upstairs anyway? I can't believe they'd be upset by me, so what is there that I couldn't take? I've seen everything any hospital has to offer, including stuff in mental institutions that would turn your hair white."

He hadn't answered, and embarrassed by her outburst, she hadn't recovered her equilibrium until lunchtime, when wine and a swim put her back in a good mood.

Susan slowly returned to the present. She opened her eyes and glanced at her desk clock. It was seven-fifteen. Toni had come by over an hour ago. She must have fallen asleep. She rose, opened her door. The outer room was silent, the labs beyond, too. Palmer and the other researchers had gone.

She went back to her desk, flicked on her neuromet-ric terminal, and started to take data from Helen again. A complex tracer technique designed by John and based on brain-cell voltage differences had been programmed into the mainframe to enable it to dis-tinguish between learned experience and other brain activity. Studies showed that during learning, the brain established a system by which regions of it cooperated. "How" was what Susan was after. A reference library of scientific papers had been programmed into the Eclipse and she decided to check out what research had been done on the subject by others.

She asked for a list of published papers. Authors' names began printing out on her terminal—Galambos, Glivenko, Kivanov, Ruchkin, and Villegas—along with titles of their works. She only had to press a key and the printed word of the work itself would appear.

Suddenly her breath caught. She leaned forward sharply.

John Flemming's name was there, along with the title of the paper the computer said he'd written.

She felt the blood drain from her face. She heard the heavy thudding of her own heart. She had a feeling the world had stopped. She put the computer on "hold" and stared.

It couldn't be. But it was. And there was no way Palmer or anyone else could have ever learned of it or known about it. The paper referred to had never been published or even revealed. John Flemming had written it at home one night and then torn it up. Only two people alive could possibly have known of it.

Herself and John Flemming.

She hadn't given the work to mainframe, and John couldn't have. He'd died and she'd buried him. Hadn't she?

12

Light rain, almost just a mist. A soft whispering envelope that cloaked everything in velvety gray.

The quiet Pennsylvania country churchyard with rhododendron bushes under spreading elms. Worn writing on old tombstones and the sweet smell of freshly mown grass.

The yawning seven-by-three-foot grave, its dark earth damp. The coffin bronze and covered with flowers, waiting to be lowered. Quiet mourners with somber faces, dark clothes.

"Earth to earth, ashes to ashes, dust to dust, in sure and certain hope of the resurrection to eternal life."

And afterward, dry sandwiches, tea, coffee, and sherry at John's mother's house to fortify those weakened by the immediate presence of death—untimely death which made their own seem urgently imminent.

At no point had it ever crossed the mind of any who participated in John Flemming's funeral that the body which occupied the coffin was not John Flemming's or that perhaps within the unbreachable and sealed confines of the cold bronze coffin there was no body at all.

To the world, John Flemming had died and was buried.

"Miss?" A voice that was persistent. "Miss?"

Susan finally looked away from her computer terminal. One of the security guards stood in the doorway. It was the night man from the lobby door down the hall. "If I'm not at my desk when you want to check out, miss, have a quick look in the cafeteria. I'll be going for coffee." He winked.

That meant a quick round of poker with the other guys, Susan remembered. Friday nights were pretty quiet. "Sure," she said, and winked back.

He disappeared. She was alone again.

But not alone. Because somewhere in the building— on the third floor, surely, where she'd never been allowed—was John.

For a few moments before the guard had come, her mind had stopped. John was dead. Then, green letters had poured across the opaque surface of her terminal screen, and John was alive. She felt first pain, then numbness, as though someone had struck her a hard blow which spread to her whole body. She couldn't move, it was hard to breathe, her heart raced.

She knew now that she had nearly fainted. The room around her had appeared far, far away, as though seen through the wrong end of a telescope. The numbness had increased, her limbs were lead, she could feel nothing. Until the security guard had appeared.

When he left, the numbness ebbed slowly. In its place, she began to feel fear, an awful gut anticipation of something so dreadful she wouldn't be able to face it. She wanted to run. But couldn't. It was the kind of fear she'd felt when seeing John's ghastly burned body, a fear that came from a helplessness to control the inevitable. Why hadn't they told her about John? Why the charade? Why were they hiding him?

Why? Why?

And how could he be alive when he'd been so close to death? When Michael had told her he would die? When she'd seen John herself and known he couldn't live? Why, unless there'd been some sort of miracle? But then, what sort of miracle?

The green words stared at her and gave no answer.

Susan finally rose from her desk. She had to talk to Michael. He had to tell her the truth. Or Katherine did. Or somebody. They had to tell her.

She went out into the silent hall and tried to control her body. She was shaking from head to foot. She saw no one. She took the elevator downstairs and went to Michael's office. It was in darkness. Katherine's too. Gladys's typewriter was covered. There were only the luminous numbers of Gladys's digital desk clock. The time was seven-forty-five. That was impossible. Where had time gone? She glanced at her wristwatch. It said the same. Had she been sitting and staring at her terminal for thirty minutes?

She went to the telephone. Michael had gone home early and might still be there. Then she remembered he wouldn't be home. When she'd turned down his invitation to go sailing for the weekend, he'd said he'd take the boat down to the James River, where he had friends. She put the receiver back.

Where was Katherine, then?

She went to Katherine's office, flicked on lights. Hadn't Katherine said something about New York? There was nothing on her desk calendar. And back at Gladys's desk, there was nothing either.

Suddenly Susan knew she didn't want to talk to Katherine about John. Or ask Katherine anything. Something about Katherine had always troubled her, some strange nagging anxiety never clearly understood.

There was only one person to talk to, and that was Michael. But how? Drive down to the James River, try to spot his boat somewhere along it from some unknown shore road? It seemed impossible. But what else could she do?

She started back up to the research division. And then, just outside the office shared by Toni Soong and Al Luczynski, she stopped short. Something had caught her eye, something she'd almost missed. She had seen it as she first walked by on her way to Michael's office, but it hadn't registered then and almost hadn't now on the way back.

Toni Soong's white medical smock lay across her secretary's typewriter where she'd slung it, obviously for some reason in too much of a hurry to go into her office to hang it up.

But it wasn't the smock itself that arrested Susan. It was Toni's identity card. She'd forgotten to unclip it and take it with her. Toni had number-one security clearance; the card gave her access to any place in the building.

Susan unclipped the card from the smock and slipped it into her pocket.

13

The card was plastic, two and a half by three inches with Toni's photo, name, and registration number occupying the top half. The bottom was taken up with dark vertical lines of varying length which when decoded by an electronic eye became keys.

It was just like her own card, except to Susan, standing by the elevator, it felt awkward and oversized in her hand.

She was still trying to understand her fear. Coming down the hall, she'd realized it wasn't just fear of what she might find. It was also fear of being caught. Guards with guns, signed statements, the U.S. government—it all now seemed totally menacing. She tried to estimate what they might do to her if she were caught. Imprison her? Realistically, perhaps not. Over the last three weeks she'd formed the distinct impression that they considered her work on John's alternate-area theories almost vital to their research. The thought was comforting.

The elevator arrived, she got in, hesitated, then firmly used Toni's card to order it to the third floor. Brazen it out if you're caught, she thought. Don't tell anyone you've got Toni's ID. Let them think Michael had yours adjusted.

The door whispered shut, confining her in the elevator's silent interior. It started upward. The floor-indicator light flashed "2." Some of the security guards were there, in the cafeteria having coffee. Then she remembered Henry Palmer. Where was he? He had the weekend duty and she hadn't seen him for hours.

The second-floor light flashed off, the third-floor light flashed on. The elevator slowed, stopped. The door opened onto a quiet lobby where there were plants, the faint medicinal smell of a hospital, and a security desk. The guard was nowhere to be seen.

Susan looked at the names on the sign-in sheet. She recognized only nurses Michael or Katherine had mentioned. But Henry Palmer's signature was there too. She'd hardly seen it when she heard a sound and a woman came into the lobby through a door marked "Ward One." She was dressed in germ-protective clothing, green surgical pants and smock, plastic boots covering shoes, a hood with a face plate.

Susan held her breath. But the woman seemed to take her presence for granted. She turned down a corridor leading from the lobby and almost immediately slipped her identity card into the security access slot at another door. When it opened, she stood halfway in it, speaking to someone.

Intuition told Susan it could be Palmer, and she finally moved. There was a bathroom just to the left of the elevator. She stepped into it quickly and held the door ajar so she still could see down the corridor.

In a moment the woman left the doorway, followed by another figure. It was indeed the neurologist, his slight frame and grandfatherly face recognizable in spite of the protective clothing he also wore. Talking casually, he and the woman came back to Ward One, and they both disappeared again.

For the first time, Susan remembered Michael saying that the third floor had two sections—Ward One, which was surgery, and Ward Two, where the ECs lived.

She left the bathroom, crossed the lobby, and went down to where Palmer had been. It was indeed Ward Two. She started to slot Toni's identity card, then remembered she wasn't wearing protective clothing. She would probably be stopped by the first person she encountered.

Across the corridor she found a small locker room. She took pants, a smock, plastic covers for her shoes, and a face-plated hood from a locker and geared up. When she had also put on surgical gloves, she went back across the corridor to the Ward Two door.

At the last moment, she almost lost her nerve. Her heart thudded, her throat turned dry. What she might discover was suddenly a terror. It was like opening

John's grave and finding what would have been there a year later if he had really died.

At the last moment, she wanted to tear off the clothing she'd just put on and run forever, from Michael, from everyone. From John, too. She almost wanted John dead again and her life to be the secure new one she'd started to build for herself, a new apartment, a new job, a new love affair. Not this. Not a nightmare beginning with the casual flick of a computer key, the zip of green print across an opaque screen.

She pushed the card into the slot. The door clicked open.

The room she entered was small. Medical monitors were crammed in with hospital cabinets and trays, with studio tape recorders and with video monitors. Observation windows looked onto two rooms beyond, both now in darkness. One room seemed to be much smaller than the other.

A young man sat at a control panel with banks of switches and buttons softly illuminated by a night lamp. He also wore protective clothing but he'd taken off his hood. His name plate said he was an RN. He looked up at Susan. There was no recognition in his eyes. Only questions. Who was she? What was she doing there?

She tried to think. He wouldn't know she'd used Toni's card. He would presume she had entry rights just because she was there and dressed for it.

She bluffed. "Hi. I'm from research. I have to see Flemming."

"Sure. Go on in. He's probably figuring out his

next step in driving everyone nuts before he goes nuts himself."

There was a door to each room, and over each a red warning light. That meant they probably opened into germ locks so the rooms beyond would remain hermetically sealed. The lights would be to show when the locks were occupied and to bar further entry.

Susan hesitated. Dread had suddenly half-paralyzed her. She knew she had to move; the young nurse had turned toward her questioningly. But she couldn't.

Then she got a grip on herself and went to the door to the larger room.

"Wait a minute." The nurse's soft voice was like a shout. "He's still in the lab. They left him there to cool off, I guess. He was upsetting the others again." He glanced at his console. "And I'd better give you a little light. We're in twilight rest, but I can up it twenty percent, okay?"

Susan nodded. "Sure."

The nurse's fingers brushed a dimmer knob. The dark beyond the window of the smaller room lightened faintly, outlining vague shapes she couldn't quite identify.

She went into the germ lock. It was lit by antibacteria fluorescents, a glow of purple in the darkness. She hesitated a last time, then pushed the next door open blindly, closing it quickly behind her and leaning back against it.

And somehow found the courage to look.

She was in a small low-ceilinged place. There

was an impression of pure cool air with a faint medicinal smell. There were scattered groups of pulsating red and green lights, a low hum of electrical machinery. And more familiar things—a row of special neurometric computers, a graphic computer "blackboard," a computer terminal.

Then her eyes adjusted and she saw the face.

It was a man, pale, gaunt, hair close-cropped and thin, eyes dark sunken hollows. He stared intently back at her.

Was it John?

She said his name. A whisper. There was no answer.

He didn't move. Three slender curved rods of polished steel, glinting faint indirect light from the honeycombed ceiling, seemed to hold him rigid. They curved out and down, then joined two upright chrome poles projecting from some sort of massive console below, its polished steel-and-chrome surface broken by dials and switches.

A coldness rose in Susan, an unspeakable horror.

She could see a face, a head, but not a body. A spark of hope flared for a split second, went out.

Between the head and the console there was a kind of pleated rubberized collar, too narrow and far too long to be a neck.

There was no body.

She stifled a scream, her hands thrust out protectively. She stepped back.

There was no body, there was just a head.

And when its lips framed her name she knew beyond doubt that it was John Flemming.

14

She wanted to run, couldn't. Her feet were lead. She wanted to scream; her throat was sand. Her mind formed words; she couldn't speak them.

She heard him say, "You shouldn't have come." The voice was electronic, a monotone. And yet, there was inflection, another tone remembered. "Or worked here. Ever." A bitter tone suddenly. "Go. Go and forget everything—what I am, what you've seen. Go and forget. Now."

It was John. And yet it wasn't. Who was it, then—inhuman but human just the same? Some kind of monster from the grave, a disembodied head, ghastly in its isolation: decapitated, guillotined by the surgeon's scalpel, and set atop the awful long pleated tube which hid the unimaginable amputation and the wires and tubes connecting it to machinery.

A head on a pole, nothing else. Executed, held aloft and still horribly alive. A life on a thread, and instant death if the thread broke.

"Susan?" The eyes changed. A brief pleading look flitted across them. "Can you answer me?"

She heard her own voice finally, strangely harsh, as though it belonged to someone else. And from a great distance. "No! Oh, no, no."

And saw her hands outstretched rigidly before her, blurred outlines in the twilight. She felt a wave of nausea and half-turned to escape, moving by instinct through an open door she'd sensed behind her. It led to the larger room.

An impression of lights and lines from medical monitors, the low hum of electric machinery, the same pure cool air, the same medicinal smell.

And suddenly another impression. Of people. Of cold appraising eyes and of minds, far beyond any ordinary intelligence, judging and weighing her.

She forced herself to look, saw them. Five heads, nothing more. Just heads.

Five more like John, semicircled in open cubicles, the surgical tongs glinting, curving up to hold each head rigidly fixed at the temples and the rear base of the skull's occipital; the long narrow pleated tube fitted to just below the chin and descending to the massive console below.

She looked from one silent face to another. There were four women, one man. Gaunt, pale, lips colorless, eyes hollow, hair close-cropped, living death's-heads.

A voice suddenly. A woman, black, middle-aged with a Medusa crown of electrodes rising from her smooth-shaven skull in a twisted rope of multicolored wire that entered the wall behind her.

Dignity and authority were in the electronic monotone. "Susan, get a grip on yourself. Susan!"

Susan faced her. The eyes softened. "I'm Helen, Susan. You know me. Don't be frightened. Of us. Of John. He didn't ever want you to find him. Don't hate him."

Through the open door, Susan could still see John's pale face and haunted eyes. And knew she couldn't run. Not now. It was too late.

She went back slowly to him in a dream and finally spoke. "You're not dead." Inane, but all she could think of to say. It seemed everything.

His mouth formed a faint smile. "No. Just half."

She fumbled for more words. "Your name came up on my computer. The article you wrote at home and threw away."

Surprise, then remembrance clouded his eyes. And immediate remorse. His flat colorless voice fell almost to a whisper. "Of course, and only you ever knew about it. I forgot. For just a moment I forgot. Vanity. Stupid, stupid."

Susan burst out, "Why, John? Why did you do this?"

"Do what?"

"This! What you are! Why!?"

He stared, then said, "Perhaps I didn't. But then I must have, no? We're all volunteers here." His face twisted abruptly into something like a snarl. "Who'd want to turn down the chance to be a genius and not be bothered by a stupid body? Be just a thirteen-pound skull full of hotted-up brains and have the chance to disgust people. I do disgust you, don't I?"

"John, no!"

"Of course I do. Look at you! Want to unzip my collar and see my stump with all the tubes sticking out?"

It was too much. The room swam. Susan fumbled blindly for the germ-lock door. John, whom she loved, or had, but not John. John, but some kind of a monster at the same time.

She pulled the door open. The voice abruptly changed, became tired and gentle and resigned. "Go home, Susan, and sleep. Sleep and try to accept. Then come back. I need you. You will come back, won't you?"

Her eyes met his and for the first time she felt him human, a somebody. She nodded. "Yes."

Some of the terror abated then. The room around her became clear. Reality returned, where she was, how she'd gotten there, Toni's identity card, the security guards in the cafeteria playing cards.

And the realization. She'd known for days that John was alive, known but kept the knowledge hidden from herself. Known because of the work which had been pouring into her computers, ideas, formulas, theories no one could be capable of except John. Not Palmer. Not herself or anybody. Just John Flemming.

Her terror had not been of finding him alive. Her terror had been in discovering what he'd become, the dread helplessness felt in the presence of the fatally injured.

"Yes," she repeated. "I'll come back."

On the other side of the germ lock, the nurse

didn't look up when she came out. He had his hood on now and was busy at the central panel. She hardly saw him. She muttered a good-night and left.

When the door closed behind her, he turned and raised his hood. It wasn't the nurse. It was Henry Palmer. He at once picked up a telephone. "She's come out. Let her leave the building." He hoped letting her go had been the right decision. He could only think that keeping her there might have shut the door forever on regaining her cooperation. He glanced at his watch. It was eight P.M. Katherine had said she was taking the ten-o'clock shuttle to New York. The plane left from National Airport, not far from her home. She might still be there. "And get me Dr. Blair," he said. "Immediately. Try her night number."

He hated himself for what he was doing. It went against his grain to turn anyone in, especially Susan. And especially to Katherine, of all people. But he had to. If he didn't, it could all come back on him. Waiting for Katherine to answer, he silently cursed the nurse for being an officious idiot. When he'd discovered Susan wasn't supposed to be there, he'd written it in ink in his logbook, and there was no way now to cover up.

Katherine's voice came on the line. Palmer took a deep breath. As he began to tell her what had happened, he switched a tape onto telephone standby. A control room audio watch was kept on the ECs. It didn't extend to John Flemming's tiny lab, but the tape would let Katherine hear what the other ECs had said to Susan, and Katherine would want to hear every word.

15

Getting out of the germ-protective clothing in the locker room, Susan was violently sick to her stomach and again downstairs after she returned Toni's ID card to Toni's white medical smock. She found the security guard in the cafeteria and he accompanied her to his station to check her out.

"You look kind of shaky, miss. Are you all right?"

"Yes, thank you. Good night."

"Good night, miss."

The drive into Washington seemed to take seconds and at the same time an eternity. She was aware of leaving the lab building at the end of its quiet cul-de-sac, of getting into her car, of sitting awhile before she felt strong enough to start it, of driving the twisting maze of macadam roads winding among the other NIH buildings, of turning into evening traffic on Wisconsin Avenue.

After that, everything was a blur of lights and cars. Questions shouted in her mind—why had no one told her? how had they hoped to keep the deception going? how long would John live now? —and remained unanswered.

Oh, God. John, poor John. It couldn't be, but it was. She'd seen him, talked to him. And those others, heads, nothing more. Except tubes and wires and machinery.

She stopped at a light. It changed from red to green, to red again and green once more. Horns shrilled. Headlights flashed. She neither heard nor saw. She tried to add it all up and understand. Someone she loved, dead and buried and grieved over, alive again, but in a sort of ghastly mockery. Only a head, a helpless gruesome medical experiment. A stranger, yet not a stranger, like some awful unexpected echo.

She couldn't think further, didn't want to. She felt completely shattered. Some other drivers shouted. She started off again.

But stopping at another light, she experienced a new wave of horror. It seemed to ride the back of her neck like electricity and rise in her chest at the same time. Suddenly she remembered John saying he wasn't a volunteer—not in so many words, but meaning it. She tried to be rational. It just wasn't possible. Michael would never have done this to him against his will.

She found herself on her own street and pulled up. There was a dark blue Porsche parked just in front of her door, its dashboard lights silhouetting a driver. For a moment she hoped by some miracle it was Michael. But she knew at the same instant that it couldn't be he; it was the wrong car.

She'd begun to shake almost uncontrollably. It had started as a slight shivering and soon it had overtaken her whole body. When she crossed the sidewalk, her legs were like jelly and she didn't think she'd make it. She felt she was going to be sick again.

Then the lights in the parked car flicked off and someone got out to intercept her.

"Susan."

It was Katherine. She was in a shirt and jeans, her hair damp. She looked as though she had rushed from a shower—so out of character Susan almost didn't recognize her.

Katherine said, "Henry Palmer just called me. He said you were in Ward Two and had seen John. I came right away. Oh, Susan, I'm so dreadfully sorry." She seized Susan by both shoulders. "Are you all right? No, you're not, you poor thing. You've had a terrible shock and you look like death."

Susan said numbly, "You're supposed to be in New York."

"Well, I'm not. Do you have any brandy upstairs?"

Susan let herself be escorted to her apartment. She found an unopened bottle of Remy Martin among the various bottles she'd salvaged from the house on Sixth Street, vaguely remembering that it had been brought by Michael to the party she and John had given. Watching Katherine pour for both of them, she felt grateful for the concern Katherine was showing. She hadn't thought her particularly capable of caring, had never quite trusted her. Now, somehow, it seemed all right to. She wondered how Palmer had found out.

She found herself saying, "John's name showed up in the mainframe's memory. A paper he once wrote. That's how I knew. It was never published. I guess he was just being whimsical. Or vain. He's . . . he was like that. So I . . . borrowed Toni's ID card—"

"Don't try to talk now, Susan. You've got to have a lot of questions, and the best thing for you would be to have them answered."

They sat on the floor by the pine table with sawed-off legs and Susan drank some brandy, feeling it run down her throat and some of her strength come back. She had to cope somehow. It was a nightmare, but so were a lot of other things. You couldn't just give up. She had to think of John, not herself. She made an effort and found courage to try to imagine what he must feel like, what it would be like to be just a head, a helpless half-being whose every need was in the hands of others. She passed her hand wearily over her face. John couldn't do that. John couldn't brush his own teeth or scratch or do anything. He could only look out at the world through those dark eyes, the captive windows of his mind, all that was left of him. Look and think and observe. And rage helplessly. That and await death a second time.

She heard Katherine say, "Maybe I should start at the beginning. Back when Michael was on staff at the hospital where I was doing my internship, they brought in an accident case one night who wasn't going to last long no matter what. Michael had the nurses in the palm of his hand and the patient had no relatives, apparently. Al Luczynski was there, too, doing his residency, and he and I found ourselves assisting in Michael's first human severance. The man only lived forty-eight hours—we didn't have the drugs we have today or the precision equipment. But Michael later did two more, derelicts who were terminally ill, and they each lived two or three weeks. Michael became fascinated by their increased mental ability. It meant the human brain could possibly double its potential. He went to Borg-Harrison. Admiral Burnleigh had just been appointed chairman and he grasped the implications involved right away. The economics, the politics, everything.

"That was five years ago, and we were doing fine until Burnleigh's board of directors hit the roof when we ran way over budget. They gave us a year to produce or else.

"You can imagine what this did to Michael. He was frantic. He saw years of work going down the drain. Then he thought of John and what he was doing with alternate-area development. If he could somehow talk John into joining him, together they might pull it off. But he never got the chance. John had the accident."

Susan suddenly remembered the party, John's flailing arms, the look on his face as he berated Michael for his secrecy. She said numbly, "John wouldn't have shared his work with Michael, Katherine. Ever. Not with all the secrecy here. Or ever volunteered. I can't believe he would, and he said he didn't."

"I know," Katherine said. "But he did, and you must try to accept it. He was completely lucid when Michael talked to him. Security or no, he decided this was a last chance for his AAD theories. He signed a standard organ-donor contract with a special EC clause. You can see it anytime you want. We still don't know why he's blocked it all out. It's probably some form of postoperative amnesia. I've tried every drug going to help beat it, but no luck. To make it all worse, at times he can be very hostile about it."

"But he said nothing to me at the hospital," Susan protested.

Katherine shook her head. "We tried to get him to, Susan, honestly. Even though we have a strict rule against it. You were different. You shared his work. But he was adamant. He kept saying, 'You bring Susan into this and I stop thinking!' "

Katherine paused. She poured Susan some more brandy and said, "Look, Susan, tell me. Are you really all right? I mean, outside of shock, how do you really feel? Not how you think you should, but actually?"

Susan found it impossible to say. She thought of Michael. Yesterday, today, she was in love with him. Could she still be?

She gestured helplessly.

As though reading her mind, Katherine said quietly, "Michael's happened in between, hasn't he? That must make a difference." When Susan looked up quickly, she offered a gentle smile. "Oh, I know you both keep it totally professional at the lab, but it's been pretty obvious just the same."

Susan was instantly cautious. So much for careful deception. The only thing to do, she thought, was to act as though Katherine had said nothing. No matter who knew, she didn't want to talk about herself and Michael.

"Whatever your rules," she said, "or reasons, it would have been better if Michael had told me right from the beginning. Told me everything."

Katherine said, "I guess at the beginning he didn't dare risk frightening you away. None of us did. Then, when you and he became involved, I supposed he kept quiet out of care and concern." She added, "Obviously it's something you'll have to discuss with him."

Susan found herself thinking of John's funeral and his grave in the little country cemetery outside Philadelphia. The tall shading elm trees, the rhododendron and azalea bushes, the fresh mown grass, the worn old tombstones, some with inscriptions you couldn't read anymore, people forgotten forever and known only to time and eternity. She tried to hold back rising bitterness. "What's in John's grave?" she asked. "Or is there anything?"

"John's body," Katherine replied. "Does that make it worse or better?"

"I think worse. But it's something I'll have to live with, isn't it? How long will this second life of his last?"

"That depends on him," Katherine answered. "On whether he can resign himself and adapt. He's in less of a revolt every day. If you could face seeing him again, work with him, it would help."

"I don't know," Susan said. The thought of going back to the lab and reliving the whole awful experience seemed suddenly overwhelming. "I just don't know," she repeated.

"Of course you don't," Katherine said quickly. "And you shouldn't try to. Not now. Now you shouldn't do anything but rest."

In a few minutes she got ready to leave. "I can stay if you want."

"I'll be all right."

"Are you sure?"

"Yes."

Katherine wrote down her home phone number. "Even if it's just a bad dream, Susan, call me. I'll come right away."

Susan promised. Looking at the number, she missed the expression that crossed Katherine's face for one fleeting second as she waited.

It was a look of unrelenting hatred.

If she'd seen it, it might have told her she was right about a thought she'd had a few minutes before.

After Katherine had gone, Susan sat a long time finishing another brandy. She felt a kind of deep-down-inside cold she'd almost never felt before.

While Katherine was telling her about John's decision to "volunteer," a vague memory, long buried, had surged up in her mind. Her cousin had come to take her away when her parents were killed. They were driving out of the farmyard, headed for her cousin's home in town. The old family dog was standing mournfully by his favorite shade tree and she'd turned to look back at him a last time, when her cousin said, "The people taking him will be here in an hour, Susan. We've found a really lovely country home." But it was a lie. Her cousin didn't want the dog around her house, and the police had come and shot him.

She'd never forgotten the expression in her cousin's eyes. She thought she'd seen the same expression tonight when Katherine had said John suffered from postoperative amnesia.

Or was she just imagining it because of what she knew about John himself? He had always objected to the use of either drugs or surgery in medical experiments on people. He drew a firm line at electrode stimulation. "Go any further than that, Susan, and you end up with Nazi experiments in death camps."

Perhaps in the face of his own imminent death, he'd changed his mind. Most people would.

But the cold in Susan wouldn't go away. If she were right and John hadn't volunteered, then there might be others who also hadn't. If that were true and it ever got out, Katherine or Michael, even Burnleigh himself, would be in serious trouble. The brain-research program would almost certainly be closed down and the millions already spent on it lost.

If anyone decided she might talk, what she knew of the program could put both her and John in deadly danger once his research was successful and they were no longer needed.

The cold in Susan grew into a kind of terror that she forced down. She was being paranoid. It was all supposition. She didn't know Katherine was lying. She only thought she might have been. She had to keep herself under control and not let her imagination run wild.

She finished her brandy and sat for a long time trying not to think. But she couldn't help it. She thought of John, the nightmare that he had become and the worse nightmare that he must suffer. She thought of Michael, the way she had loved him. She wasn't sure she ever wanted to see him again, but she knew she had to. Facing Michael was the only way she could face the ghastly horror of what her life had suddenly become. Until she listened to what he had to say, she couldn't make any judgments or draw any conclusions about anything.

It was nearly dawn before she fell into an exhausted sleep.

16

There was a public telephone at one corner of Susan's block. Katherine immediately used it to call Burnleigh's office. He was at a State Department reception for the visiting president of Brazil, but he always wore a beeper. The night operator would contact him and he'd call her back. While she dialed, Katherine momentarily gave in to chagrin. She'd turned down an invitation by Burnleigh to accompany him and his wife to the affair because of the New York conference. Now she was in neither place.

When the operator answered, she read off the phone's number by the faint light of a streetlamp, said it was an emergency, and hung up to wait. She could see lights still on in Susan's apartment and hoped she'd succeeded in calming her. A man walked by, seedy, wearing a raincoat. He looked her over, then to her relief, walked on. It seemed forever before the telephone rang. She yanked the receiver from its cradle.

"Katherine? What's up? I thought you were in New York."

"I canceled." She told him briefly what had happened and explained where she was.

"Sounds as though you handled it right, but we'd better meet, discuss options just in case." His voice was toneless, betraying nothing of what she suspected he felt. "Why not join me here at State?"

"I'm not dressed for it. Henry Palmer got me out of a shower."

"I'll come outside, then. I think I'll recognize your car."

"A dark blue Porsche."

He laughed. "Yes. Pretty fancy!"

Katherine went back to the car and drove down C Street to Twenty-third and the executive courtyard entrance to the monolithic mass that housed the Department of State. She parked, told the security guard who she was and whom she was waiting for, and then waited, watching the doors and imagining the reception. Burnleigh had said it was in the Adams Room. She'd been there once, seen the priceless Early American antiques, John Adams's famous desk. Some of Washington's most important people would be assembled there tonight, a glittering array of administration officials, many of Washington's foreign diplomatic corps and members of the House and Senate as well as high-ranking officers of the armed forces. Black tie would be in order and the women would be in evening dresses and expensive jewelry they'd taken from safe-deposit vaults for the occasion.

When Burnleigh appeared in the door in a tuxedo, she flashed her lights. He came and got in beside her.

Characteristically, he wasted no time. "Okay, no point in recriminations. Tell me first, how the devil did she get up there?"

"For a start, Flemming listed a paper he once wrote in the mainframe's memory, one that only he and she ever knew about."

"On purpose?"

"Apparently not. Apparently, it was just an ego trip. Then she got hold of Toni Soong's ID card. Toni's overtired, she left it in her office. We've all done it."

He shook his head. "All right, we'll figure out a future fail-safe for that one. Now, personnel. Who's who this weekend?"

"Dr. Palmer has the duty. I believe Toni is at home."

"Where's Michael?"

"On his boat."

"Have you spoken to him?"

"No. I wanted to report to you first."

He nodded. "Good. What's his reaction going to be?"

"I don't know." She said it as calmly as she could. "He's been having an affair with her."

Burnleigh cursed under his breath. "I should have thought he would know better."

"It could be to our advantage."

"Explain."

"When I talked to her, I had the feeling she wasn't

as upset about John as she might have been if she weren't involved with Michael. She seemed more shocked by what John is than by having him return from the dead, so to speak. And by the fact that he never told her he was 'volunteering.'"

"What did you say about that?"

"I told her postoperative amnesia had made him forget signing an organ-donor contract."

"And?"

"She seemed to accept it."

He was thoughtful a moment, then said, "Okay, we have two options. Get rid of her completely or keep her on under heavy surveillance."

"We have to keep her. We need her."

"Do you think she'll want to continue?"

"I suspect she will. But that, again, may depend on Michael."

"Okay, we'll put people on her at once, have her phone monitored, all that. They'll need to get into her apartment, of course, when she goes to work Monday, to get her private address book and see who her friends are. Tomorrow you might pick up any such information she may have at the lab."

"Certainly."

Burnleigh glanced at the dashboard clock. "I left Eleanor with the Portuguese minister of foreign affairs, and his English is appalling."

He opened the car door. "I want you also to contact Michael. Tell him I'm sending a helicopter. I'll see him tonight."

"Yes, sir."

"Will there be any problems with Luczynski or Soong?"

Katherine thought of them both—Luczynski the smiling bear you were never totally sure of, Toni always inscrutable—but she couldn't see how Susan's discovering Flemming could possibly be a threat to either. She said, "I don't believe so."

"I'll leave them to you. Palmer does what he's told, you once said. What about nurses, technicians?"

"It really doesn't concern them. Susan's new ID card will make her freedom acceptable."

Burnleigh got out, bent toward the window for a last word. "You've done a good job, Katherine. Sorry Michael strayed."

She shrugged, managed a smile. He slammed the door and walked away.

She lived at Watergate in the South Wing, closest to the white facade of Kennedy Center. To her it was more than a prestige address, it was a centrally located convenience, and if you could afford to live there, why not? Her apartment was three rooms near the top floor, with a balcony view of Theodore Roosevelt Island across the Potomac.

She drove the Porsche into the underground garage, nodded at the night security guard who knew her well, took the elevator upstairs, and getting out at her floor, went down the silent carpeted corridor to her door, readying her keys.

Her apartment was spacious, a blend of modern furnishings and provincial antiques, with raw-silk drapes and upholstery and deep pile carpeting, all put together by one of the capital's leading decorators. She fixed herself a Scotch, went into her bedroom. Taking off her moccasins, jeans, and shirt, she sat on the bed and dialed a number. She felt exhausted.

Toni Soong answered, voice slightly slurred. Katherine guessed she'd been drinking. There was background music and someone saying something, probably Sara, she thought. She'd known about Toni a long time, and it didn't seem strange to her. Katherine had had the occasional encounter with women herself before Michael. She also knew she could have Toni anytime she wanted, although Toni had never made an embarrassing pass. She'd sensed it the night they'd all swum nude from Michael's boat.

"Toni, it's Katherine." She told her what had happened and how Susan had gotten upstairs.

"Oh, shit. Jesus!"

"Don't feel badly about it. She had to find out sooner or later."

"Well, maybe, but just the same . . ."

"I've talked to Michael," Katherine lied. "We're just going to play it cool, proceed as though nothing had ever happened."

When they'd hung up, Katherine glanced at her bedside digital clock. It was five past ten. She imagined Toni, slender in a flattering pajama ensemble, her delicate face softly made up for the evening, young Sara blond and lovely at her feet. She had a strange feeling, suddenly, that none of it would ever be the same again for any of them.

She dialed the marine operator and gave her

Michael's number, praying he was on board and not ashore.

The number answered, a man's voice. "Hello?"

"Hello. This is Dr. Blair. I'm looking for Michael."

"Oh, yes. You must be Katherine. I'm Charley Phelps. We're all just coming back from dinner at my place."

Katherine remembered Phelps vaguely, a big florid man who had constant indigestion and something to do with the St. Michael's yacht club. She suddenly felt an outsider.

"He's just pulling alongside now with my wife in the other dinghy. Will you hold?"

She waited. Michael finally came on the line. "What's up?" He sounded vaguely annoyed.

She told him straight out and almost with pleasure. "Susan got to Flemming with Toni's ID card."

"Oh, my God. Where is she?"

"At home. I've just left her. She's all right. We'd all better hope so, anyway. But Burnleigh wants to talk to you. He's sending down a helicopter."

"When?"

"Right now."

There was little else to say. Did Michael hear the coldness in her voice? She didn't care. She'd tried a shot in the dark with Susan, pretending to know about Michael and her, and Susan's reaction had told her everything. She wondered how many times they'd been to bed. She closed the conversation abruptly, put the receiver down, and sat thinking. Burnleigh was right. She'd done a good job. And if she could just keep on top of things, they'd get out of this yet. She drank down the Scotch, made another, and finished the shower interrupted two hours earlier.

Drying herself before the full-length bathroom mirror, and afterward generously applying body lotion, she liked what she saw. Her femininity pleased her, the high contour of her breasts, the flatness of her stomach, her slim hips and thighs and her skin, tanned and blending with the copper color of her hair. Everyone said she had a beautiful body, and it was true, she did.

She thought about Michael and Susan. He'd be back in Washington within an hour. Burnleigh would read him the riot act and tell him he had to keep Susan on the team no matter what. Michael would join her afterward, probably before midnight.

The jealousy that had become a dull nagging misery to be kept repressed somewhere deep inside suddenly flared. She fought it back, trying to think of herself from a professional point of view. What, after all, was jealousy except personal insecurity, the threatening of your basic self-image? Thinking of Michael making love to Susan was painful only because it put her at risk. But was there really any risk to her, ever? Susan McCullough might be lovely, she thought, and good in bed—she'd have to be, to satisfy Michael. And Michael in turn might be doing everything to her he could do to a woman to make her never want another man but himself. In spite of all that, however, women were secondary to Michael. What came first was his work. If it came to a choice between Susan and the EC project, he'd choose the latter.

Then, Katherine knew, she'd have him back again, perhaps permanently. She was generous with cologne, finished her Scotch. When she went to bed, she fell asleep almost at once.

17

It seemed the phone had been ringing forever. Then Susan realized it wasn't the phone. It was a completely different sound and nothing like the phone. It was her door buzzer.

She sat up, confused as to where she was and feeling completely drugged. It was daylight and she at first thought that she'd fallen asleep following lunch. Then she realized she was undressed and the sheet was pulled up over her. She looked at her bedside clock. It said eleven-thirty-five.

She remembered everything then. It all rolled back over her in sickening waves. In the oblivion of sleep, she'd forgotten.

The buzzer persisted. She listened until it stopped, got up, slipped on her light summer robe, and went to the kitchen. She tried to understand how she felt, couldn't. John, the horror of him, Katherine—it was all a jumbled dream, with herself somehow an onlooker, involved but not involved. The only thing she knew was that yesterday she'd been leading one life and today life was entirely different.

She'd begun to make coffee when the telephone on the kitchen counter rang. She stared at the phone, knowing intuitively it had to be Michael. Last night she'd been desperate to talk to him. Now the moment was here, she felt in a panic.

Finally she answered. He sounded vaguely accusing. "I rang your doorbell forever."

"I was asleep."

"And telephoned first. I thought something had happened. Your car was here."

She wanted to protest. She could have gone somewhere without her car, on foot or in a taxi. But she let it go.

She heard him say, "Susan, Katherine reached me. We've got to talk."

And heard herself stalling with invalid excuses: she wasn't really up yet; she had calls to make. Until she realized how ridiculous they were. She told him she'd be down in a few minutes and put back the receiver without waiting for him to answer.

She finished making coffee, brushed her teeth, took a shower, then put on makeup and dressed in a casual summer skirt and blouse and slipped on espadrilles.

She had no idea where they would talk; she only knew she would feel trapped if he came upstairs. Looking out the window, she could see the sun diffused above the heavy, hazy polluted air of the capital. Leaves on trees seemed limp and the street was silent. It was going to be a scorcher.

She went downstairs. He was waiting at the curb and had put down the roof of his convertible. Their greeting was awkward, as though neither wanted to be the first to speak.

Susan took refuge in the mundane, trying to organize her thoughts. "I have to go to the supermarket."

He didn't protest. They drove the dozen blocks in silence. She'd forgotten it was Sunday and the supermarket was closed. It left her feeling defenseless and she suddenly wanted to cry, and because she did, she felt a rush of anger. With herself, with Michael. With everybody. Anger and defiance. God damn the whole goddamned rotten world. And made up her mind. Stop being defensive. He's vulnerable, too.

They sat in the supermarket parking lot, not moving. Michael finally asked her, "Where to?" and she tried to think. The heat was almost suffocating. The backs of her thighs stuck to the seat; the tightness of her bra straps was oppressive; her hair fell about her neck like an unwanted blanket. She thought of Michael's lovely old boat, swimming naked off it in the delicious cool of the Chesapeake, and then she thought of afterward, of lying on deck making love, sometimes in the moonlight, the whisper of dark water around them and shore lights twinkling, sometimes in bright midday, both their tanned bodies glistening with water and sun oil, Michael slowly driving her to delirium. She thought of their making love once standing against a mast, her arms tight around his neck and her legs locked around his waist, both of them laughing like children and crying out wildly in sheer ecstasy when they came at the same time and not giving a damn if anyone on a passing boat saw them.

She'd been so in love with Michael, time had nearly stopped.

Then she thought of John. Tubes and wires and the sweet-sour pervasive smell of medical antiseptic; the heavy electric hum of the machinery keeping him alive; the sickening gurgle of the pharyngostomy drain; his pale gaunt face, eyes exhausted hollows, his hair convict-short.

The anger rose in her like wind. Out of town, the heat would be bearable.

"You'd better run me home. I have to go to Philadelphia."

"I can drive you. What's in Philadelphia?"

She laughed, but with her voice only. "John Flemming's grave."

She could see it hit him. It was almost a physical blow. She could see it in the sudden warnings in his eyes and a tightening around his mouth. He didn't answer and she didn't say more.

They drove up I-95 in silence. Washington's bad air fell behind them and the sky cleared just as she'd thought it would. The breeze became sharp where it touched her bare arms and legs. Just before the Delaware Bridge, they branched north in the direction of Wilmington and after a few miles turned off again for Chadds Ford on Brandywine Creek. The countryside became soft and welcoming with fields and pastures. They stopped at a roadside stand for flowers and in a short time reached the village where she'd always thought she'd buried John. The graveyard lay behind an old white clapboard church which fronted a quiet country road.

Everything was familiar—John's grave, the graves to each side and those beyond, the branches of giant elms scattering warm sunlight into lacy patterns of cool shadow over old stone and fresh-cut grass. The flowers she'd put there two weeks ago now were withered away.

The grave of a stranger, she reflected, was as meaningless as the inscription on its cold headstone which said who lay there but failed to dispel the person's anonymity. A grave of someone you loved, however, had a unique and very personal quality.

Which kind was John's? Was he still down there, far below the mossy grass, confined to an eternity in the inky blackness of a bronze coffin? Or was that nobody now? Was a person's being all in the head, the body meaningless? Didn't you really need both?

She had no answers. She wondered if anyone ever would.

She turned suddenly to Michael. It was time to talk. He was leaning rigidly against one of the elms a few yards away, his eyes looking blankly inward on his own thoughts. She wondered what they were.

"Why did you do this to me, Michael? Just tell me why. And to John."

At first she didn't think he'd heard her. He kept staring at nothing. But he suddenly looked down and said, "We needed him. Desperately." There was an edge of annoyance in his tone, as though he thought her question unfair. "And he agreed."

"To a living death? I don't believe it."

"Some ECs see it as life. When they'd expected to die. I talked to him and he signed a donor contract."

"John said he didn't."

He flared. "Dammit, I don't care what he said. I have it with me." He pulled a sheet of paper from his pocket and shoved it at her.

She scanned the lines of small print. It was a standard organ-donor form with a special paragraph for volunteer ECs. John's scrawled signature was at the bottom, and unmistakable. Was her suspicion of Katherine groundless?

A sudden new suspicion took its place. She couldn't suppress it. She handed the form back to Michael and said, "Did he know what he was signing?"

Michael flashed angrily. "For God's sake, Susan, what sort of a bastard do you think I am?"

She flashed back instantly, "The sort of bastard who kept it all a secret." All her held-back hurt and anger came out in a rush. "Jesus Christ, what do you suppose last night did to me? And this?" She gestured helplessly at John's grave. "I buried him here. In a coffin. All winter and this spring I came and put flowers where I thought he was, and last night, all of a sudden I find he's not here at all, only part of him is, and the rest of him is being kept alive on some goddamned machine in a laboratory."

This time when she started to cry, she didn't try

to hide it. When Michael put a hand out to her, she flung it off. "Why didn't you tell me? All the time we were making love, you knew he wasn't here. You were seeing him, talking to him. And letting me think he was dead. Oh, Christ, I can't stand it. How could you ever ask me to come to work for you? I was okay. Why didn't you leave me alone?"

He sat down next to her. After a few moment's silence he said gently, "I'm sorry, Susan. We needed you, too, as desperately as John. You know that. I should have told you, of course. It seemed tough, even rotten, not to. But I couldn't risk your maybe not joining us if I had. First I thought we could get away with it; then you and I became personally involved. That was the last thing I ever expected and I lost my nerve. That's the only way I can explain it. The longer I put off telling you, the more impossible it became. I couldn't face what I knew it would do to you, especially not when I was responsible for the way John is."

"How about what you might have had to face yourself from me?"

She wanted it to hurt him and she could see it had. He looked away and shrugged. "That, too," he said.

Susan could find no further words. His explanation was almost exactly the same as Katherine's. She fussed with the flowers she'd brought John and then rose. "I'd like to go back now."

On the return trip, they were silent again. There were still things to be settled. She waited. The road seemed endless. He didn't speak.

When they were entering Washington, she said, "Michael, thank you for taking me up there." She said it to force him to speak.

He gestured. "Sure." He hesitated, then asked, "Susan, what do you want to do?"

Her heart turned over. It was what she'd waited for.

She drew him out. "Do? What do you mean?"

He said cautiously, "About work, I mean. And John."

She let a moment go by before she replied. Then she said, "I'll be in tomorrow."

"You don't have to, you know."

"I do, don't I? For his sake." She avoided his eyes. She didn't want to see the relief that had to be in them.

"I can't answer that for you," he replied. "Just don't do anything you don't want to."

"When may I see him?"

"Anytime. I'll be operating in the morning. Can you handle it by yourself?"

She nodded. "Yes. I'd rather see him alone the next time, anyway."

Ten minutes later, they pulled up in front of her door. Susan didn't get out at once. She sat looking down the empty street, now partially in late-afternoon shadow, and tried to reframe her thoughts about herself and Michael.

She said, "I don't know about us, Michael, you and me. I need time to think." She put hope into her voice.

"You've been through a lot, Susan. I understand."

She turned to look at him. He seemed drawn beneath his suntan, and his eyes and expression were somber. She wanted to reach out and touch him. She didn't. It was too soon.

At John's grave when she'd finally cried and Michael had come and sat next to her, she had also wanted to touch him. Even more, she'd wanted his arms around her. In spite of everything, the magnetism he exerted over her had unexpectedly been there again, all the old chemistry. She would have forgiven him everything right then except for a strange lingering suspicion she couldn't explain. A deep-down feeling that he still wasn't being completely open with her. At the same time she'd wanted him, she'd felt uneasy, vaguely frightened of him and in danger.

Nothing about him back there in the cemetery explained to her why. He was the old Michael, the man she'd given herself to and still wanted. And yet, he wasn't. He was different.

But in the silence on the way back from Philadelphia she had suddenly understood.

Now she said, "I guess we both have—been through a lot, I mean."

She got out and didn't look back when she went into her building.

In her apartment, she suddenly felt exhausted. She fixed herself a drink and then remembered that she hadn't eaten since lunch the day before. It took effort to make herself a sandwich—she felt her whole world was destroyed. But she forced herself to. While she ate it, she looked in the newspaper to see what movies were around town. She found one she'd wanted to see for some time and went out.

It was all part of the role she'd made up her mind to play. She was going to pretend she'd completely accepted John, the EC program, Michael's keeping it a secret from her. She had to convince everyone that she was a trusted and eager team player.

She was going to make believe she didn't know Michael was still lying to her. Because he was.

Coming back from Philadelphia, she'd begun thinking about Katherine again. Nothing Michael had said or done, not even showing her the signed donor contract, could erase the memory of Katherine's expression and her own sense that Katherine was lying. She'd suddenly realized it had to mean Michael was lying too, and that meant he probably wasn't being open with her about anything else, either.

When he'd become angry about the donor contract and John's signature, she'd almost been taken in. It was so natural. Maybe *too* natural. All the way home, her sense of danger had increased. Wasn't there something odd, also, in the way both Katherine and Michael had come rushing to her?

It might not have been just to justify their making John an EC. It could also have been to see how much of a threat she was likely to be.

Even if she were wrong, no matter what she felt for Michael, no matter what magnetism or chemistry still remained, she didn't dare trust him until time and events disproved her suspicions.

Her own life was one thing. John Flemming's was another. He was helpless and he had to be protected at all costs.

18

Monday morning. The operative procedure began at precisely seven o'clock.

The surgical team was comprised of Michael, Toni Soong, and Al Luczynski, along with two circulating nurses, a scrub nurse and a profusionist who would monitor the heart-lung machine. Three hours earlier, the patient's head had been shaved and washed. She'd received Pentothal as an induction procedure, then had been anesthetized with halothane and nitrous oxide and her brain barbiturate-blocked.

She was young, only twenty-two, and had been on her college varsity swim team. Three weeks ago she'd misjudged a dive and landed back on the board, breaking her neck. When Katherine had first learned of her, she was suffering partial pulmonary paralysis and a tracheostomy planted in her throat was hooked up to a respirator. She was a borderline case with a slightly better than fifty-fifty chance to live. With the exception of John Flemming and Claire (and Katherine didn't really count Claire; there had, after all, been extenuating circumstances there) the young diver was their first nonvolunteer.

Katherine was pretty certain no one on the surgical team knew. A forged "volunteer" signature she had obtained in a supposed interview during Michael's absence seemed to satisfy him, and she believed a skillfully dummied hospital chart along with other rigged records would keep Al Luczynski in the dark, as well as Toni, and persuade the surgeon that anxieties she'd expressed about the patient being in "pretty good shape, all things considered," were unfounded.

Katherine had learned of the young woman's accident and subsequent medical history courtesy of HEAD—a coincidental acronym for Hospital Emergency Assistance Data. A computer network shared by capital area hospitals, it had long been the principal source of their ECs.

She had expected difficulty in getting the young woman to the Borg-Harrison operating table but had found it was actually quite easy. In big-city hospitals, a patient can disappear and be registered as dead with little notice from anyone. Hardened intensive-care nurses watch over scores of the dying and take little interest in anyone no longer under their supervision. To operating nurses, a patient is anonymous, and overworked resident doctors can easily be persuaded of the need to transfer a difficult case to a special facility.

Thus the job lay mostly in eliminating or falsifying official information. This was achieved by the basically simple process of using access codes to manipulate computer records.

Now the patient was ready. Toni made the first incision into the skin of the neck just above the clavicle, where a thin red line had been drawn earlier while the patient was still in pre-op. She next directed her scalpel through the superficial cervical fasciae and into the platysma. Within minutes, both she and Michael were cutting through the sternomastoid and the strip muscles, the sternohyoid and the omohyoid.

Michael felt dead tired and his mind was not really on what he was doing; his head was still filled with the accelerated events of the past forty-eight hours and with the confrontation he'd had with Susan. Ever since Katherine's phone call had shattered a weekend carefully planned to avoid any emotional demands, he'd begun to regret having taken his research to Burnleigh and Borg-Harrison five years ago. If he'd kept it going in some obscure provincial hospital, slowly raising money to improve his own equipment, he might well, he thought, have arrived at equal success.

He mechanically ran his scalpel through a final section of an omohyoid and heard Toni ask for clamps to tie off the bleeders. The moment the carotid arteries and internal jugulars were exposed, they would hook them into the pump oxygenator of the console, which would sustain life in the severed head. The complex mechanical heart-lung would begin immediately to take over the function of the soon-to-be abandoned body organs of the patient.

146

Simultaneously, a dialysis machine in the same console would assume kidney function and a nutrient pump begin to infuse the head's bloodstream with total parenteral feeding. Finally, in order to make electronically assisted speech possible, a specially designed pump would be activated to supply pressurized air to the larnyx, now tucked up into the truncated esophagus.

His mind wandered again. After Katherine had reached him on the boat, he and Charley Phelps had gone back ashore and lit the front lawn with headlights from several cars. Twenty minutes later they'd heard the chopper coming in high and had barely spotted its green and red running lights before it plunged quickly down like some huge and ominous night bird.

The return to Washington and Borg-Harrison headquarters on Massachusetts Avenue had been a blur of anxiety as the darkness of St. James Bay rapidly gave way to the sprawling rhinestone glitter that was the nation's capital at night.

It was not so much Burnleigh's anger, however, that upset Michael; he'd seen flashes of that through the rimless tinted glasses on other occasions, and it had rarely disturbed him. It was more the sudden realization that he'd lost Burnleigh's support. Every man had his breaking point, and the admiral's had obviously been reached. Burnleigh had clearly decided to cover his own flanks.

"Katherine says you're intimate with the lady, so you'd better use every bit of influence you may still have in that department."

It had done little good to tell Burnleigh that if he hadn't become involved with Susan in the first place she probably never would have agreed to join Borg-Harrison. The admiral had only become more coldly insistent, and it rankled.

The fact that Katherine knew about him and Susan rankled even more. Had he and Susan been so obvious, or was it just intuition on Katherine's part? Her coldness on the phone had annoyed him. Dammit, she didn't own him. Worry that Burnleigh might find it unprofessional if they married, and thus possibly injurious to the EC program, wasn't the only reason they hadn't. There'd always been some other hesitation on Katherine's part for reasons she'd never disclosed.

While Michael thought, he and Toni worked in silence. Besides the hum of the pump-oxygenator, the only sound was the clink of steel instruments as the scrub nurse handed them one by one to both surgeons. The clink of steel and the endless metallic snap of clamps shutting off vein after vein. At the surgical trolley, the circulating nurse kept unwrapping more clamps, more retractors, more scalpels, more forceps, sponges, bipolar cauteries, and suction equipment.

Once Toni looked up and her eyes met Al Luczynski's. She wondered if he was thinking of their conversation on the beach. He stared back with what she thought was a kind of defiance, although she could see only his eyes and might be mistaken. She returned to work and forgot about it when Michael sharply pointed out a slipped clamp and called to the scrub nurse for more sponges.

It was the forty-seventh head they had removed from its body and they'd been at it for nearly three hours, with some of the biggest work coming up. They'd cut through the esophagus along with scores of minor muscles and venal systems; the vertebral artery was attached to the pump-oxygenator. Work could now begin on the microsurgery area of the cervical column with its twisted maze of critical nerves through which the brain ran the body and in turn received messages from it. Using an operating electron microscope and a special fluoroscope hooked into a TV monitor, Michael prepared to sever all final contact between head and body, thus rendering the body useless.

Although from start to finish the entire operation was carried out nearly automatically, two and a half hours after they'd begun every member of the team was drenched with nervous sweat.

A quantity of blood sufficient for the needs of the bodiless head had been diverted to the pump-oxygenator, and the naked body itself was now drained of remaining blood and put first in a body bag, then in a plastic container. Within half an hour the container would be delivered to an undertaker who was on Borg-Harrison's payroll. He, in turn, would eviscerate it, stuff the visceral cavity along with the anal and vaginal orifices with cotton, pump the arterial and venal systems full of formaldehyde, and finally put it in a sealed coffin.

In spite of their hardened attitude toward death,

disposing of the body was a moment most of the team hated. Now, as always, the lifeless splayed legs, the exposed female genitalia suddenly become so sexless, the flaccid breasts, and the flopping arms of the freshly decapitated corpse seemed somehow still alive. And yet there was, as always, the jarring absence of anything above the shoulders except the raw, bruised meaty stump where the head had once been. One nurse turned away.

Toni now quickly and skillfully attached the Gardner-Wells tongs, driving their sharp points through scalp incisions into the holes she'd bored in the outer table of the skull at both the base occipital and frontal holding places. The circulating nurse swabbed the areas of entry; then the head was carefully positioned over its life-sustaining console, the tongs slotted into their holders and adjusted.

The operation over, the head was irretrievably joined to the machinery which was its new body and which would be its sole connection with life until it died. Still deeply anesthetized, it rested quietly, its eyes closed and with the usual faint liquid sound coming from the pharyngostomy tube placed in its throat to draw off excess saliva when the operation began.

Michael and Toni joined Al Luczynski to watch the vital-signs monitor and to cross-reference its multilinear reports with the dials of both the pump-oxygenator and the cranial-pressure pump. The head's blood pressure was 100/80. Intracranial pressure was 5 Torr. It was read through a catheter Michael had sunk into a lateral ventricle of the brain itself. At the same time, he had inserted a temperature probe and the reading was a normal 37° C. They also verified arterial blood gas. It too was normal. The p^h was 7.2, the $p^{co}2$ thirty-five, and the p^o eighty-eight.

While Michael was finishing the severance of the spinal column, Toni had attached scalp electrodes to the shaven skull. The EEG watch would be constant for the next ninety-six hours. Currently it showed almost entirely beta waves, signifying relative brain inactivity.

After about ten minutes at the monitor, Toni went to the recovery room to check it out prior to bringing in the head on its console. Michael left for an adjacent locker room to take off his surgical clothes. He removed his mask and cap and leaned wearily against a locker before taking off his surgical gown and pants. More than anything, he wanted to go home and sleep. It was not so much physical tiredness, he knew, as a need to escape; to get away from Burnleigh's needs; from Katherine's insistence on adherence to research deadlines he never should have agreed to; to forget the mess he was in because Susan had discovered Flemming alive.

When he'd seen her yesterday, he'd somehow managed to tread a fine line between the falsely accused innocent and the anxious and contrite lover. It hadn't been easy and there'd been some bad moments. When she didn't at first answer the phone or the doorbell, his imagination had run wild. She'd taken an overdose and left some kind of disastrous note for the police; she'd somehow ducked Burnleigh's surveillance and left town and would reappear some-time in the future, protected and accusing. A dozen things.

Her silence on the drive to Philadelphia was an equal trial. It had been hard to keep silent also and play a waiting game. It had been even harder to hide his relief when she said she'd come back to work.

When Katherine had managed to get Flemming's signature on an organ-donor contract without Flemming realizing what he'd signed, he'd worried it might somehow come back to haunt them. But it hadn't so far, and now he thanked God for it. If he hadn't shown Susan a contract, she probably never would have come around.

Even so, he still wasn't totally confident. In spite of her obvious attachment to Flemming, there was still the off chance that seeing him again might trigger some new and adverse reaction in her. It was going to be a trying week.

Coupled with all that was the vague and nagging guilt she made him feel. Somehow he'd let her get under his skin far more than he'd ever planned, and that wasn't good. It wasn't just the sex which was so good, there was something else about her, a kind of willful independence and lack of guile which intrigued. And unlike Katherine, she never demanded.

He jarred back to the present. He ought to visit her now in her office. He needed to keep making sure of her.

He'd started to take off his gown, when he heard the scrub nurse cry out. Something in her tone made him return at once to the operating room. Toni was already there. She and Al Luczynski, along with the nurses, were mutely staring at the new EC.

Everything during and after the operation had conformed so completely to previous experience that no one was prepared for the young woman's sudden death only minutes after they had stopped monitoring her. It was already too late to apply any emergency resuscitation measures.

Michael was stunned. "What happened?"

If one of their ECs died from postoperative causes, it was acceptable to him as being within the demands of the program. But death during or because of actual decapitation was not. It meant that somehow they'd slipped up. So far, they had lost only six that way.

He heard Toni say carefully, "I don't know, Michael, but I think we ought to suspect an embolism."

Al Luczynski said, "I'll second that."

Michael knew they were probably right. He glanced at the vital-signs monitor. The EEG showed no reading at all. He pushed a recall button on a controlling computer. It replayed the moment of death. The brain-waves line showed normal vertical movements, then abruptly went flat. It was just as though someone had pulled an electric plug.

He lifted one of the head's eyelids and touched the pupil. It was fixed and dilated, with no reaction. It certainly looked like an air embolism. But how?

He stepped back, surprised at the anger he felt. "Damned thing," he said. "One mistake and they snuff out like a candle. No wonder Katherine has so much trouble with their going nuts. All right, Toni, remove both halves of the brain as soon as you can. We'll have to autopsy it just for the record." He kicked the console. "And someone better check out this bloody thing. See if there's a leak somewhere."

It was a gesture. He knew it was very likely that he was the one responsible. Operating on only two or three hours' sleep, you made mistakes. Along the line, perhaps hooking up an artery to the pump-oxygenator, fatigue might have caused him to let a substantial jet of air into the system. It was bitter. They needed every head they could get.

He went back to the locker room. By the time he'd finished changing, the scrub nurse had unfastened the tongs holding the head in place and was draining its blood into a sink prior to putting it into a plastic carrybag. Al Luczynski had disappeared someplace, but Toni Soong was still there, not looking at the head but staring off into space. She looked white and drawn. Michael knew he ought to say something to her, make her feel it wasn't her fault, perhaps even admit it could have been his. Toni was always the first person to blame herself for anything untoward in surgery.

But somehow he couldn't. To hell with her, he thought. To hell with everyone.

When he got down to his office, he told Gladys he didn't want to see or talk to anyone. "That includes Burnleigh," he said. "I'm out." He closed his door hard behind him.

Outside, Gladys wondered. She'd never seen him in a mood like that.

Several doors down and some minutes later, Toni Soong also shut herself in. She felt a kind of guilt she'd never experienced before. The dead woman's chart hadn't fooled her for one moment. What was on it hadn't quite matched with what she'd seen in the patient. Before the operation she'd had the deeply disturbing suspicion that they were about to destroy the life of someone who still had a chance to live. And with that, she had the even worse suspicion that perhaps there had been others about whom she'd been unaware.

She'd forced suspicion from her mind: neither Katherine nor Michael could be capable of such a thing, no matter how desperate they might be for new ECs. But now she wasn't sure. Someone had died, either by her hand or Michael's—it didn't make much difference whose.

She wondered how Al Luczynski felt. Or Michael. Or if they felt anything. She wasn't sure they would.

Suddenly she realized she wasn't sure of anything anymore.

19

As Michael was leaving the operating room for his office, Susan was paying her second visit to John in his tiny neurometric lab adjacent to where the other ECs were, in what she'd learned was called the "homeroom."

The meeting proved nearly as painful as the first. From the moment she came through the inner door of the germ lock, it took everything she had not to reveal again her shocked dismay and near-revulsion at his ghastly appearance. She couldn't reconcile what she saw with the John she'd loved, lived with, shared her body with. And she continued to be terrified that he would suddenly fade out, without warning, right before her eyes and be dead again.

With a sinking heart, she knew he saw right through her attempt to hide her feelings. Like Helen and the others in the homeroom, he seemed to have developed almost superhuman insight. She tried to think of what to say to him and couldn't. She was certain that no matter how careful she was, the anger and hostility she'd experienced at their first meeting would be directed at her again.

And suppose he again claimed he hadn't volunteered? She couldn't let him think she didn't believe him. At the same time, if anyone else thought she did, especially Katherine, it would ruin the image she was trying to create of not being a potential threat to the program.

Keep calm, she kept telling herself, keep calm so you can think clearly. Just don't upset him, whatever you do, whatever he says.

She wasn't worried that she and John might be overheard. He'd told her that the computer-jammed little neurometric lab wasn't wired. They could talk freely. What worried her was that under the influence of drugs, he might be indiscreet.

To her surprise and relief, however, he said nothing. Perhaps it was too painful for him, she thought. Nor was he in any way hostile. Instead, he displayed a kind of gentle consideration for her misery and insisted they get to work right away.

Was it remorse for having mistakenly let her know that he was alive? It didn't make any difference. Susan complied. Work was a welcome escape and she disciplined herself to think of nothing else, as though John were completely normal and she wasn't living in a nightmare. Within two days they achieved a lot, rapidly developing a new program of deep electrode stimulation, first for Helen, then for a second EC, Thurston, a white male in his late fifties who had sat on the federal bench in Chicago before a terminal illness.

The experiment was complex. Scalp electrodes swarmed over the ECs' shaven heads, and both had electrodes sunk deep into the periaqueductal gray, a learning area of the brain between the third and fourth ventricles. Two more electrodes were planted into the hippocampus close to the temporal-lobe cortex and one into both the left and right thalamus far down near the brain stem where it came up from their necks. Since the brain has no pain receptor of its own, they could not feel them.

At John's command, each electrode would stimulate with several milliamperes of electricity. He'd learned to use a "tongue-toggle" switch and a "sip-puff" tube, both standard to quadriplegics, which were lowered from a ceiling module. With a flicking motion of his tongue or a tiny burst of air, he could broadcast ultrasonic orders to a control unit commanding thirty-six apparatuses ranging from all his neurometric computer equipment to direct audio communication with whichever EC he was currently working on.

Routine and familiarity telescoped the rest of the week. It flew by, and suddenly it was Friday. At the same time, it seemed to Susan years since she'd discovered John; it seemed he had always been the way he was now. The confusion she'd felt at his grave was gone. The massive and complex machinery sustaining his life became to her his body.

Throughout the week, she only saw Michael when

he came once to her office to discuss work with her and Henry Palmer and when he paid his daily visits to the ECs and to John. The first time he appeared in John's lab, she felt anxious and disturbed by the effect he still had on her in spite of her continuing suspicion of him. Hiding her storm of divided emotions was at first difficult, and at times Susan wondered if she even half-succeeded. It was like love-hate. She was drawn to him and simultaneously frightened of making one false step that might give her pretense away. She had to be warm and friendly and yet not so much as to upset John, whose disdainful and cynical barbs whenever Michael joined them showed only too obviously his deep and rebellious resentment at what Michael had done to him.

As far as the others were concerned, she was surprised when no one, not even Toni Soong, ever mentioned the illicit use of Toni's ID card. She wondered if such casual behavior by her colleagues was deliberate, or whether no one was as upset as she supposed. She found it strange. Strange and worrying.

She kept up a pretense with them all that she was to be trusted, that she'd weathered the shock of discovering John alive and was taking it in her stride. While she did, she tried desperately to figure out what to do. Should she try somehow to blow a whistle on the lab, and if so, to whom? If she did, wouldn't that person be bought off or silenced in turn, with herself in dead trouble for nothing? Burnleigh was a powerful man with easy access to the Oval Office and almost anybody else in Washington.

Was it worth the risk? Nothing could restore John and the others to what they had been. Their condition was irrevocable.

Besides, there was Michael to consider. She knew it was useless to try to get him to change the program or anything in it. His lies to her aside, it was his life's work and it was obvious he saw nothing wrong in it. Regardless of what he had done to John, would it be fair to wreck him as well? Or even to judge the morality of the whole EC research program? Others, with different points of view and different priorities, might assess it differently. At times, she felt completely confused.

With a jar, Susan saw by a digital wall clock that it was now five-forty-five. She and John had worked for more than three hours with the ECs. John had already charted brain responses to light flashes and electronic sounds and now was doing a final recording of answers to verbal challenges, each response appearing as lines of jagged green on his EEG monitor, to be classified simultaneously against a preestablished norm by the Eclipse mainframe, which also translated it into a series of workable numbers and stored the results for future study.

Susan was at the microcomputer, feeding in figures. Looking back from the clock, she saw that John was staring at her, half-smiling.

Out of the blue, he suddenly said, "You know, we really ought to talk about your affair with Michael. I don't mind you having one, of course—how could

I? But I can clearly see it's weighing heavily on you."

It caught her completely off guard. She started to stammer a protest, but he stopped her, the emotionless electronic monotone of his voice somehow making what he said even more poignant. "Susan, this is one of those moments when a head would give its life to have a body. I'd like to reach out and take your hand. Better than words, that would say it's okay, you don't have to hide Michael from me."

When she could bring herself to look at him, she could hardly see him. Her eyes were filled with tears. "I'm sorry, John."

He suddenly seemed the old John of long ago. "Sorry? What the hell for? He's an attractive man, although not exactly my type, and you're a warm and vital young woman." His smile was cynical and amused at the same time. "You could hardly have a romance with me, could you? So come on, get off the guilt trip and forget it."

"I'm afraid it isn't that easy."

"Oh?"

Susan studied him. He seemed detached, objective. Certainly he didn't appear to feel sorry for himself. She wondered how much she could tell him, and decided not much. It wasn't that she suddenly felt an adulteress. It was more not wanting under any circumstances to transmit her fear to him. She said, "I don't know anymore how I feel about him."

"Because of me?"

"Of course."

"My existence shouldn't have anything to do with

it. When you first became interested in him, I was 'dead.' Remember?"

"I can't handle his not telling me the truth."

"Under the circumstances, I'm not sure I would have either. And ruined my chances of getting you. He's human too, Susan, believe it or not."

It was so decent, Susan impulsively brushed her gloved hand against his forehead. Because of her protective hood, it was the closest thing she could do to giving him a kiss.

"I love you, John," she said. "Please don't ever forget it. I always did and always will."

"Whatever you do, Susan, be careful of Katherine. Hell hath no fury."

"How do you mean?"

His eyes widened. "Everyone knows about her and Michael except you, apparently."

Then she understood, and everything instantly fell into focus: Katherine's strange look of hostility when they'd first met; her own instinct to avoid her; Katherine's kindness and warmth of the other night when Katherine in fact must hate her. Why hadn't Michael told her that Katherine Blair was the casual woman in his life? Of course, Katherine had to have been lying to her, and that confirmed all her worst suspicions of Michael. A door in her mind slammed shut but she didn't have time to think further. She saw John's eyes flick sharply. Simultaneously she heard a low moan from the adjoining homeroom.

John said quickly, "You should go now."

It was too late. The moan rose to something like the howl of an injured cat, inhuman and awful.

Susan turned.

"Susan, no!"

But she was already running to the homeroom.

The first thing she saw was Peggy, the youngest EC. Her face was contorted into a ghastly grimace. Her eyes rolled. Her teeth bit her lower lip. Blood ran. She seemed more rodent than human.

The ghastly sound kept bursting from her mouth. Helen's electronic voice got through it. "Peggy, it's all right. We're here. Don't cry, we're here." Her eyes were frantic. And helpless.

It was too late. The interior germ lock flew open; two nurses, then Katherine, appeared.

Judge Thurston said quickly, "Don't take her away, Katherine, please. She'll get better if you just let her rest a few days. Please."

Katherine favored him with a brief professional smile, then became aware of Susan. The smile froze.

"I'm afraid I'll have to ask you to leave, Susan. Don't worry. It's just hysteria. We'll have her calmed in no time."

It was quiet, authoritative, the order of a doctor in charge of a life.

Susan went back to John. His face was set like stone. His electronic voice said, "Do as she says." He closed his eyes, shutting her out, but just before he did, she saw in them a look of naked fear.

She had seen the same in the eyes of the others: Helen, Thurston, Rachel, and Annette. She glanced back at them. Katherine had taken a small vial from her pocket and had upended it into an injection receptor in the life-sustaining console beneath the stricken woman.

The howl rose to a piercing scream. One of the nurses was slipping a germ-protection hood over Peggy's head.

Susan left. She had a feeling she would never see Peggy again.

20

When the door closed on Susan, John watched Katherine in the other room administering tranquilizers to Annette, Rachel, Thurston, and Helen. His eyes followed the nurses as they wheeled Peggy away.

To where? None of them had ever known where you went after your mind had gone. Where had they taken all their predecessors?

To some soundproof someplace where their screams and howls would disturb no one? Or to some awful execution—doctors and nurses expressionless and unreachable, eyes removed from life; professionals disposing of an experiment no longer worth bothering about? No ceremony, no good-bye, no last cigarette, no prayer. Just hushed medical jargon or perhaps not even that. Perhaps just arranging to meet for coffee or talking about weekend plans.

Then casually, a flicked switch, darkness. Forever. One life less. Yours.

His eyes returned to the germ-lock door, mute emphasis to Susan's departure. His computer-packed room seemed empty without her. But just a week ago when she had come through that door for the first time, his mind had railed at being so exposed, so vulnerable, so helpless to stop her. And he had been filled with guilt and chagrin for having, for just one instant, indulged his ego by claiming authorship of that stupid, meaningless paper he'd never thought anything of in the first place. Go away, damn you. I'm not what you used to hold so close at night. Go away!

When the pain of being discovered and of seeing her horror had died away, however, he'd made up his mind never again to tell her he hadn't volunteered. He could only pray she hadn't heard or had forgotten or plain didn't believe him. It was too dangerous. One misstep on her part and she'd have a fatal accident someplace, or worse, she'd end up on a console the way it was rumored a rebellious nurse once had. They couldn't afford to take any chance she'd talk.

Poor Susan. What a mess he'd gotten her into and what hell it all must be for her.

A century before that, she'd stood by an elevator and smiled as she had today. "I love you, John." He remembered himself. He'd still been a man then. Dying, but still human, still John Flemming. Someone to love. Not a hideous non-man, something to shudder at.

The elevator door had closed on her, the elevator had moved. Afterward, just impressions. A drugged haze. Corridors, an ambulance, strange nurses, a room somewhere. A coolness on his head, a burring noise. And the young woman doctor's face and amber eyes. Smiling.

"We're giving you a haircut."

Someone else calling his name. "Can you hear me?" It was Michael Burgess. He wore a cap and a surgical gown.

Bursting glare then. Overhead lights. Nurses, doctors. A big bearded face. "Just breathe normally, Dr. Flemming, and count with me." The hissing anesthesia cone. Rubbery. Counting, floating. Darkness and violet light, next red and green. Kaleidoscope.

"Six . . . seven . . ."

Spinning, falling. A leaf.

From far, far away on a roaring wind, a vague humming sound. And a voice. "Wake up, John. Wake up." Sharp and clear. That was the young woman doctor again. Hooded, but face clear behind a wide vision plate. And another woman, Asiatic.

He'd tried to move. Legs, arms. Anything.

Couldn't. Lead weights. There were monitors with dark faces. Green lines and dots. The form of a room. He seemed to be sitting up. But how could that be? The humming sound now echoed in his head, a faint liquid gurgle vibrated his mouth. And a strange tightness was at his neck. Hands did something. A pressure increased at both temples.

Michael Burgess, then. Close. Smiling. "John, you're not going to die, we've given you a whole new life."

They went away. His descent to hell began.

First, just a reflection on a darkened window. His own. Head shaved. Next, awareness of massive polished machinery below. And a wall someplace cluttered with medical monitors.

Uneasiness.

Curved tongs held his head motionless. Why? The beginning of fear.

Where was his body? Him.

And suddenly, understanding. The great awful stupefied realization. All at once. Like a terrible blow. His body *wasn't*.

There was only his head.

And the nightmare began, the helpless vulnerability, the exposure, the terror felt at the void beneath him. Time was meaningless. Minutes ran into hours into days. The hooded doctors and nurses coming and going, the jumbled confusion of winking red lights and jagged green lines on the monitors.

Saying he lived.

But they were wrong. It wasn't he. Not John Flemming. It was just their puppet on electrode strings, nothing more. An isolated brain encased in a sawed-off flesh-and-bone coffin. A thirteen-pound medical miracle, theirs to command. For whatever, whenever.

Or so they thought.

He'd felt words finally hiss from his lips. Electronic. "I'm not John."

John had died under the guillotine, the forty-third time it fell. Before him, forty-two other tumbled non-humans. Forty-two medical experiments with no rights, no choice, no say, kept in forced consciousness by machinery anyone could shut off. At any time. For any reason. I don't like you. Flick. Good night.

Not me, friends. I'm not doing your work for you. Ever. You'd better believe that.

Enter Katherine. God's most beautiful body, the bitch. Slender, feminine, amber-eyed, and out to break his will. Cajoling, ordering, finally compelling with drugs and depth electrodes, with unspeakable mind-horror pain. A low rheostat turned just a fraction, he became anything she programmed, from a slavering orgasmic sex freak, the biggest hard-on ever, to a gibbering mindless idiot. Or drugs withheld so phantom sensations could take over; the acute discomfort of unrelieved bladder and bowels, the misery of unrelenting itches, all the thousand agonies of a long-discarded and rotting body.

But she couldn't make him create. No doctor, no science, could yet do that. And probably never would. In those ten billion intricately connected cells which made up the average human pink and gray matter, there was a microuniverse no one could ever completely manipulate, any more than man could maneuver the stars.

He'd decided the best thing was to die; to will himself into the final peace of ultimate darkness. Defied, Katherine had brought in Michael. The ultimate deity. Father, Son, and Holy Ghost. How omnipotent do you feel today, God, because I'm on my way out. Makes a real challenge, doesn't it?

All the cold clichés, then. How lucky he was still

to be alive; now he could finally realize success on his alternate-area theories.

"Sorry, Michael. It's too late. You started with a dream and you surrendered it. You weren't tough enough and the quicksand's sucked you under. To hell with all this do-good talk about raising up humanity. The quality of life cannot be judged by its quantity. If you imprison or kill just one person even to help millions of others, you've defeated your purpose. I won't be dragged down with you."

And then he'd heard Michael tell him Susan was working there. She was downstairs right at that moment, in an office, at a desk.

"I hired her three weeks ago, John, as Palmer's assistant. For obvious reasons, she thinks your work is coming from him, but I could easily set her straight." A casually triumphant smile.

"However, I don't think she could stand your dying twice, John, so whether I bring her up here to see you is your decision."

That's the way it had been. The worst nightmare come true. Of course, Susan. Who else could they get to follow his thinking if he surrendered and finish his work when he went mad or died?

They'd left and the overhead lights of his room had dimmed into twilight. A Beethoven chorale whispered from stereo speakers. He'd lost. In one shattering revelation, his direction had been forcibly turned from the peace and oblivion of death back into the agony of life.

And into a new and even more awful nightmare

because now he was no longer alone; now there was Susan.

He had to get her out of it. Somehow. She was in dead danger, of that he was certain. Had to be. To hell with her and Michael being lovers, the crucifying torment he'd suffered when after Michael had come to the lab a few times he'd sensed a strange discomfort in Susan and had begun to realize they had been and probably still were. There was far more at stake than his feelings. Susan's life could be on the line. So encourage her with Michael, the way he'd already tried to. Let her have any protection lover Michael might be able to give her. He'd seen the danger in Katherine's eyes. It wasn't just jealousy, it was ambition and her need to use Michael to realize it. When the day came for him to be taken away and Susan in turn wanted to leave, Katherine would do everything possible to stop her. She would try to use Susan to guarantee success for Michael and thus for herself. At the same time, she would have revenge.

While the massed voices of the choir rose in splendor to Beethoven's genius, he'd taken first steps in a rescue effort. He'd lipped his sip-puff tube, directing his terminal to access the Eclipse mainframe. But it wasn't for neurometrics. Alternate-area brain development could go straight to hell.

At some time, someone had programmed a special code into the mainframe's myriad maze of silicon. That code or "password," was now stored on one of hundreds of memory discs each containing millions of segments of information. The password served as a key to the computer's security lock. Without it, the mainframe remained isolated from the outside world in the Borg-Harrison building. With it, he'd be able to open a "trapdoor" to TELENET, the national computer network and hundreds of other computer nodes on the same circuit. Seconds after he typed a revelation of what the lab was doing into his terminal and ordered the mainframe to run it, the world would know the Borg-Harrison secret. And the world would act, surely, at least where Susan was concerned.

He had tried to find the password all week. During daytime hours when he was supposed to be working on alternate-area development, he'd sent a stream of programs into the mainframe, each designed to force disclosure. Evenings he'd done the same. Mainframe couldn't program itself into revelation, obviously. Security blocks obviated that possibility. Nor could he direct his terminal to program. It wasn't "smart." Someone had seen to that just in case he got any bright ideas. So he had to create the programs himself. It took time, endless time.

Tonight, he again worked feverishly. When the nurses came to wheel him back to the other room, he hadn't protested. He'd long ago learned it was useless. Besides, it didn't make any difference. They couldn't remove him from his own brain. Late into the night, while the others meditated or studied, he again created one password-search program after another and put them on hold in his own memory. Tomorrow he would recall and feed each to the mainframe. Computers didn't think, they took orders, and if a human brain had thought up the password and encrypted it to guarantee its own security, then a superbrain could decrypt it.

One way or another, he'd find the trapdoor to the outside.

sideboard.

21

Al Luczynski couldn't take his eyes from the picture. It was a large sepia nude study of two young women, half-life-size and realistic enough to be provocative although at the same time it was clearly serious art. Their gently embraced bodies seemed to float timelessly in space against the otherwise nearly bare white walls of Toni's large high-ceilinged living room.

He heard her call out, "Okay, here we are!" Not wanting to be caught interested in something so overtly erotic, he turned quickly as she came from the sideboard with drinks.

But she caught him just the same and smiled knowingly. "Do you like it?"

"It's lovely." His own voice sounded embarrassed and it made him furious with himself.

"As long as you're not shocked. Conventions create strange illusions about things like sex." Toni smiled again, teasing him. She put two drinks down on the wide polished marble table nestled in the L of a modern couch which was covered in a pale rough woven cotton.

Luczynski carefully lowered his big frame onto the sofa cushion, as though he might break something. He wasn't used to such expensive luxury. His apartment was little more than a furnished room and there'd been no money in his Detroit background. His ambition to become a doctor had meant immense sacrifices for his family, including his older sister who had given up a college education of her own in his favor.

Toni headed for the kitchen. "I'll get some cheese and then you can tell me what's on your mind."

He watched her go, guessing she was probably wearing very little if anything under the loose folds of her caftan. It added to the impression of sexuality the whole apartment gave him. A month before Susan's appearance at the lab, he knew he would have felt excited by it. Now, he wasn't so much. Now, his feelings were more clinical and Toni less the desirable and provocative woman than the sexless neurosurgeon masked and gowned in the anonymity of the formless surgical clothes he was used to seeing at work. Susan, so much like Claire, had softened much of his memory of the Toni of the lonely beach they'd visited from Michael's boat, her slim body bronzed and her breasts thrusting against the soft faded fabric of her string bikini.

Thoughts of Susan the same way were keeping him awake nights. But not just Susan in a bikini or naked in his bed arousing him with whispered love.

He thought of Susan nicely, too: of having candlelit dinners, going to movies, or walking hand in hand through a shopping mall where he would buy her something she saw and liked. These days he thought of nothing else. She was Michael's for the moment, and that hurt. But it wasn't her fault and it wouldn't last forever. Katherine would soon break it up, and then he'd have a fair chance.

Toni brought cheese and crackers and he had begun to wonder how to work up to saying what he was there to say, when she abruptly made it easier by coming right out and telling him herself.

"It's sort of what we talked about on the beach that day, isn't it? Ethics? Morals?" She laughed. "I was pretty rough on you. You should have busted my nose."

"No," he protested. "You were okay. I was just being hypersensitive."

"I don't think so, Al. You loved Claire. But just because you're such a good-natured big bear and so decent, nobody suspects you're capable of suffering— which of course you are, perhaps more than any of us."

He felt shy then, and jiggled ice cubes in his glass. "Well," he said, "it's partly that. I thought about what you said, and . . . well . . ." He shrugged, stopped. What he wanted to say seemed more difficult than ever.

"And what? You think the girl we lost on Monday maybe wasn't a volunteer either, is that it?"

He looked up sharply. Her dark Oriental eyes, slightly hooded, met his without flinching. She sat very straight and still, her drink cradled in both hands.

"That's about it," he answered. "Jesus, Toni, don't you?"

She didn't answer directly. She said, "I saw her signature on an organ-donor contract."

"You saw Flemming's on one. And Claire's, too."

Toni asked another question. "What makes you suspicious, Al?"

"Well, I just didn't get the pre-op readings I'd get from someone as sick as she was supposed to be."

There was a silence. And then Toni stared into her drink and said, "With me it was her chart."

"Her chart? How?"

"It didn't show sufficiently serious deterioration to indicate immediate terminality." After a moment she looked up, as though relieved to have finally said it. "And so she died, Dr. Luczynski."

"Yeah. She died." He sounded numb. "What about her dying? What about the embolism?"

"That could have been anyone. Me, Michael, Sara, the other nurse, the profusionist."

"I think it was Michael. He was asleep on his feet. I watched him. But you're right. Who goofed isn't important. What is important is what the hell is going on before we ever operate."

She shrugged. "Demand has exceeded supply, I suspect."

"You think she wasn't the first? And that maybe there'll be more?"

"What do you think?" She laughed harshly. It was an affirmative, not a question.

Luczynski took a deep breath. "It's driving me

nuts, Toni. Suppose it ever got out. Isn't there something we can do about it?"

"We could quit. Both of us. Lie about what we've been doing. Cover up somehow. There must be a way."

"No. We couldn't." He took a deep breath and told her what else was on his mind. "Susan's car was in the shop Wednesday. Brakes or something. I gave her a ride home. I watched her go into her building and started to drive away. Then I noticed this guy in a car halfway up the block. He was just ducking a pair of field glasses and I thought at first he was only a Peeping Tom. To make sure, I came by later at night. This time there were two guys, and again yesterday and last night."

"Are you sure it's Susan they're watching?"

Luczynski nodded. "It's got to be. I have a friend who works for Ma Bell, and he checked out Susan's line. There's a tap on it."

Toni stood up and walked slowly across the room. She stopped near the drawing of the two women, staring blankly at nothing, and said softly, "Holy fucking hell."

Presently she came back and quietly sat down again. "Burnleigh," she said. "It's got to be. That bastard! He probably has a small private army left over from his old CIA days. And of course it's Susan they're watching. When she discovered Flemming was alive, Burnleigh must have just about freaked for fear she'd blow a whistle. And he could have decided the same where we're concerned—is that what you think?"

He shrugged. "They haven't tapped our phones yet."

"They could. And if either of us quit, they could do a lot more, couldn't they?"

Luczynski said slowly, "Well, if our research program succeeds, I guess you're right. It would be worth almost anything to keep it quiet, no? The political implications of what we're doing are staggering. I mean, who the hell are we? Stupid doctors. They've got them by the million everywhere." He paused and added, "Look what happened to Claire, and all she did was say she wanted to leave."

He retreated into his own thoughts then, as did Toni. When their eyes met, it was only to communicate helplessness.

Luczynski jiggled the ice cubes in his glass again and Toni finally said softly, "Oh, my God, Al, what the hell have we got ourselves into?" For once she didn't sound confidently in charge of things.

"The end justifies the means," he replied slowly. "Any means."

Toni decided that just about sized it up. Her eyes bleakly took in the luxury of the lovely living room which was costing her so much. Then she went and got them both another drink.

22

It happened when Susan least expected it.

Another week had flown by in which she'd learned to live with nagging fear and depression. She hardly saw Michael at all and self-protectively had immersed herself so deeply in work that she almost didn't realize it. With John's increased brilliance added to the equipment they now had, they achieved some important breakthroughs on experiments they'd been working on for close to a year before he "died." Evenings, she stayed in her office until nearly midnight, going home to sleep six troubled hours, returning at seven in the morning, sometimes even earlier.

Then, at nine A.M. on Friday, Michael suddenly appeared in her office doorway and as though nothing at all had ever happened, gave her a warm smile and blandly announced they were going to New York over the weekend because he had to see someone at Columbia Medical Center. He took her coming with him completely for granted. "We'll grab the evening shuttle tonight," he said.

Almost to Susan's surprise, her "no" came easily. Ten days ago, it would not have. She would probably have said "yes" and without being motivated by fear. Ten days ago marked the end of her first week of working every day with John. Looking back, she realized now that during that week, she'd become so used to his condition that, incredibly, she'd nearly fallen into a trap of medical acceptance and callousness. In spite of her shock at discovering John and in spite of all her first fears of herself being seen as a threat, Michael's charisma and what she'd felt for him before had begun to take effect. She'd started to feel less in danger.

Peggy had abruptly changed that. The EC's pathetic and frightening madness served to snap Susan forcefully back to reality. The research program was an obscenity. John and the other ECs lived an existence of horror. And Michael had suddenly become a man who reduced human beings to howling things. The Dr. Frankenstein who had, in his quest after science, sacrificed his own humanity.

"Oh, Michael, I'm sorry. I can't."

He looked taken aback. "Why not?"

"I have two experiments I have to monitor. If I stop them, it will be days before I can return them to the stage they're at now."

"Can't you just put them on computer hold? I've reserved at the Plaza and I have tickets for a show."

The lies became almost a pleasure. "It wouldn't work. My problem is the ECs themselves. The constant flow of response is part of the experiment. I can't interrupt it for more than twelve hours. Oh, Michael, if you'd only told me yesterday or the day before."

He surrendered. "Okay, if you can't, you can't, I guess."

It was reluctant, but the sullen look he'd worn slowly faded as they went on to discuss work, and when he left, she felt confident she hadn't done any damage by her refusal.

John wasn't so sure. When she told him, his expression became somber. "I think," he said evenly, "that you should leave here as soon as possible."

"You said that once before, remember?" She touched him affectionately.

"That's when I was concerned for myself." He smiled crookedly. "For my own image. Now I'm suddenly concerned for you."

"For me? Why, for heaven's sake?"

"Why? Because you've started to reject your protector, that's why."

She laughed, bluffing. He mustn't know she understood. "Michael? Who's he protecting me against? What are you talking about?"

"Against one scorned Katherine Blair, for a start. Who else? Or have you forgotten her so soon? As long as you have Michael, you're probably safe from her. Without him, you're in trouble."

She shrugged. "Don't be silly, John. She's part of the program, and the program needs me. She's not going to do me any harm as long as it does."

"And when it doesn't?"

"If and when it doesn't and if and when Katherine decides to be a bitch ... well, I'll cross that bridge when I get to it."

"In other words, I should leave you women to scratch each other to pieces at your own volition."

Susan laughed. "In other words, yes."

John studied her from behind half-lowered lids. The same old McCullough set jaw. The same direct and defiant stare. Total stubbornness, he thought. God, what had life taught this girl who had lost everything so early? To get her own way eventually, that's what.

"You're a stubborn fool," he said.

"I love you, too."

She smiled and he gave up, knowing that if he still had a body he would feel for her all the physical manifestations of fear and anxiety, an increased heartbeat, a tightening of the stomach. She still did not seem to have realized how much danger she really was in. "Susan," he said, "just one more thing. There's something I need."

"What?"

"A drug. Phenmetrazine."

"What does that do?"

He smiled. "Basically, it's used to control appetite. That's if you have a body. If you're just a head, it would serve nicely to combat the calmative they give us. Haldol, Valium, all that 'sleep-well-and-don't-give-us-any-problems' stuff. It would give me an instant high. Make everything between the ears work twice as well and twice as fast."

She frowned. "And you're not supposed to have it, otherwise you would have asked Michael or Toni."

Of course that's what she'd say—he'd already figured that.

Why indeed not ask one of the doctors, unless they would be certain to refuse? And if they refused, it meant there had to be something wrong with the damn stuff.

"Susan, I need it."

"No."

"It's important for our work. I'm half-doped most of the time." Important? How much could he understate it? It was critical. His mind was so tired he couldn't continue without the boost the drug would give him. But it wasn't for their work. The password for the elusive "trapdoor" to the outside world through TELENET and its hundreds of other computer nodes remained nearly as impossible to discover as ever. Night after night, he had forced his overworked brain to create endless new programs to feed his computer by day. Day after day, his progress remained so slow as to be maddening. It seemed centuries since he'd switched on his terminal and begun.

"Hypothesis."

"Waiting," Mainframe said.

"You resist because you've been told to."

"Correct."

"The order was encoded."

"Correct."

"The code is in your memory bank."

"Correct."

There were four billion storage sections in the mainframe's thousands of memory discs. And he had to pry the access password loose from somewhere among them.

He had a minor break right at the beginning. "It's alpha, not numeric."

"Correct."

That meant the password was in letters, not numbers. It would make it easier to decrypt.

Next, he'd found out that the password had no user designation. They were so certain they had encoded it in such a way that nobody could find it that they had not taken the extra precaution of blocking out the curious. He was as free to ask for it as anyone else.

But from then on it was all uphill. No matter what his question the answer he received in pale green print across the terminal's cathode-ray tube was almost always "No," "Invalid," "Not possible," or "Information Classified."

In their very impersonal quality, the rejections had a personality of their own. Whoever had designed the password had little imagination or time for fun. Who was it? What nameless, faceless person hunched over a terminal like his own, fingers tapping at keys? He would probably never know.

But once in a while there'd be a cryptic "Yes" or "Continue," and he'd kept going. Only this weekend he had found the correct memory disc. What still lay ahead was a mountain. He had to find on what level of the disc the password was located, then at what extent—which meant its precise location on that level. By analogy, it was as if the extent were a country and he had to discover what was equivalent to an extension of an unknown telephone number in an unknown district of an unknown area. After the extent, he had to find the block, or area code, and within the block, the files where the number itself was located, and finally the field, the extension.

When he knew all this, he could open the trapdoor.

But starting three nights ago, he'd fallen asleep; last night, too.

And yesterday he had no longer been able to think. He'd tell his brain to work, and it refused. He was burning out, more tired than he could ever remember. There was a fuzziness in his mind which took every ounce of concentration to dispel. With each day that passed, it was harder and harder to focus on any specific thought or idea.

Phenmetrazine would change all that. Phenmetrazine was a drug which would flail the brain's lagging neurons as though with a steel whip. Phenmetrazine would be like adding ether to a car's gas tank. By the gallon.

But he had to be careful. The drug could also kill him. Overloaded neurons could short-circuit. In one massive flare-up lasting just seconds, the whole infinitely complex machinery that was his brain could go into seizure and cease to function at all.

He heard Susan speaking again. "Please, John. Try to understand."

Silly damn woman. Like a broken record. If he could only tell her the real reason. But he couldn't.

Not without revealing his terror, his conviction that she'd end up on a console. Even though she had half-rejected Michael, she would never believe him capable of setting her up to join the hellish half-limbo world of an EC.

"Please, Susan. For old times. I really need it. And trust me, I don't plan to commit suicide. Promise."

"Can I think about it?"

Ah, she was weakening. But as yet hadn't surrendered. He turned on his terminal; he'd pushed her enough for one day. "Don't think too long," he said.

He told her of some electrode changes he wanted to make on Helen and began to create a neurometric formula to incorporate those changes, which he would program into the mainframe.

Half an hour later, Susan left him and went back to her office. She suddenly felt unexpectedly unafraid and confident. Saying no to Michael and then talking frankly to John had bolstered in her a new determination somehow to resolve the mess they were in. How, she didn't know. But she knew that if she bided her time and kept her wits about her, she would find a way.

Her new, upbeat mood was shattered almost from the moment she walked through the door of her office.

The typed note, in a sealed envelope with her name on it, was neatly slipped behind the roller of her typewriter:

YOU ARE IN SERIOUS DANGER. YOUR HOME TELEPHONE IS
TAPPED AND YOU ARE UNDER CLOSE AROUND-THE-CLOCK
SURVEILLANCE. TRY TO NEGOTIATE A RESIGNATION, IF
POSSIBLE, BEFORE IT'S TOO LATE.

There was no signature.

In seconds she felt vulnerable and exposed. The
people around her became instant strangers. Someone among them knew something about her she
hadn't even known herself, or even suspected. If
she were being watched, it had to be because she'd
discovered John and was now considered a major
security risk. But why should she try to quit? Surely
she'd be a greater danger to Borg-Harrison out of it
than if she were still an employee.

Was the message a hoax? Was someone, for personal reasons, trying to get rid of her? Katherine, for
example?

Her first thought was to show it to John. But after
a few minutes she began to have second thoughts.
He was clearly worried about her as it was. Why
burden him further? There was nothing at all he
could do about it.

Twice during the morning she crumpled the note
and threw it away, only to change her mind and
recover it a few minutes later, smooth it out, and
read it once more. Who the hell was it who tor-
mented her?

At lunch, no face gave her the slightest hint of an
answer. Palmer beamed his usual grandfatherly smile.
Katherine was as coolly polite as ever, Toni as cheer-
fully inscrutable, and Al Luczynski's appraisal of

her femininity as schoolboyish. Even Gladys remained her brittle and spinsterish self behind her
slanted rhinestone glasses.

It had to be a joke, she thought, somebody's sick,
cruel idea of fun.

But looking at their faces, she knew it wasn't.
They might be many things, each and every one of
them, but they weren't the type for that. None of
them was. The note was the real thing.

23

The trouble began at three A.M., during the ECs' two-to-four A.M. nighttime free period, when they could rest, sleep, or meditate as they wished. There was an equivalent period during the same hours of the afternoon. The rest of the time, twenty hours, they were subjected to a wide range of experiments, some having to do with John's AAD theory, others involving the learning-saturation experiments they had been doing before John had joined them.

The soundproof, hermetically sealed homeroom, its air carefully regulated by humidifiers and the temperature precisely 68 degrees Fahrenheit, was silent save for the low hum of electric machinery. The artificial twilight was dotted by the pulsating red and green lights of life-surveillance medical monitors, and a piano concerto, its stereo quality muted to quiet acoustic perfection, filtered gently down from the honeycombed ceiling.

The five ECs, each rigidly held by surgical tongs

over individual life-sustaining machines, were arranged in a semicircle: Helen, Thurston, Rachel, Annette, and John Flemming.

It was a time when they usually communicated with each other in a kind of group therapy. In sharing fears and anxieties or even just mundane thoughts, they would find certain solace from the collective and personal nightmare they all suffered.

Annette, however, had not spoken at all. She seemed completely preoccupied, and Rachel, never very tactful, suddenly said, "Hey! What's with God's favorite today?" Annette was deeply religious, and Rachel, an outspoken atheist, loved goading her.

"Nothing." It was barely a whisper.

"Like hell!" Rachel's thin face was scornful. She'd been a TV journalist before coming down with a fatal cancer, and she might have bordered on beautiful if it were not for a certain sharpness of feature and an excess of feminist hostility.

"You're keeping something back," Helen observed more gently. "And we've always agreed not to do that."

Annette looked stricken. Before severance, she'd been a bank teller. Held hostage in a robbery gone wrong, she'd ended up in Michael's hands from three bullets in her vital organs.

"Do tell us," Thurston urged. "You'll feel better if you do."

"Is it because we're recorded?" Helen asked.

Annette stared, then blinked her eyes, the signal they all used to replace a nod.

"Oh, come on," Rachel said. Her eyes flashed. "Can they do worse to you than they already have?"

"They can, and you know it," Helen said shortly. "They can punish."

Rachel shut up. Like John, they'd all experienced the agony caused by a half-milliampere of electricity from an electrode planted in or next to a pain receptor. Just the way they had all been rewarded with the publicly embarrassing ecstasy of a seemingly endless orgasm.

Thurston shifted his eyes to Annette. "Do you think what you have to say is incriminating enough to warrant punishment?"

"Take a chance," Rachel said. "It probably won't be picked up."

The others' eyes followed the look she shot at the now darkly opaque surface of the observation window through which they were usually kept under close scrutiny from the control booth. They had ascertained over the months that during their A.M. rest period the duty nurse usually shut off his audio and also rested.

Words burst from Annette's lips then. "It's Peggy. She was faking. She couldn't stand it anymore. She decided wherever they take us couldn't be worse, and she put on an act. I begged her not to."

Rachel broke the dead silence that followed. "Oh, my God, the damned little fool."

"We don't know it's so terrible," Helen said.

It was obvious she was simply trying to make everyone feel better, but Rachel wasn't playing.

"Don't be stupid," she hissed. "If it's not terrible, why don't they ever tell us about it?"

"I don't think they take us anywhere," Annette whispered. "I think she's dead. I think they just kill us."

"Hush," Judge Thurston said gently. "You know the rules." First and foremost of those rules was not ever to dwell on death, so immediate to all of them. To do so produced nothing but greater despair.

John didn't speak. He was remembering Peggy as she was before she had become a frightening animal thing that howled pain and despair from a distorted face turned nonhuman. For a moment he remembered her as young, delicate, and brunette, the slender tongs which gripped her small head more like fractured halos in the soft light than cold surgical steel. And the pleated blue nylon-rubber column beneath her chin more like the ruffles of a high-necked dress than camouflage for wires and tubes and the ghastliness of surgical truncation.

And for a moment, too, he thought of her as a free and independent young woman with a woman's body and all its needs and desires, before a car accident like his own had changed all that. He wondered if Annette was right. Perhaps Peggy's final madness wasn't what she'd planned. It seemed too real to be an act.

Glancing quickly around the semicircle of massive console machinery, each machine surmounted with its tragic supercargo of half-life, he could see in the eyes of each the dull shock and sick fear felt over Peggy's fate. All the terror and identifying anxiety they'd experienced when she was taken away had returned. He wanted badly to tell them what he was doing. He wanted to explain how he was trying to crack the mainframe security code, that there was hope after all.

. But he didn't dare. Sleeping duty nurse or not, he didn't dare risk their only chance. Who knew what one of them might innocently say while drugged by Katherine?

Judge Thurston's voice broke into his thoughts. A tone of cold, almost lofty anger rode through the electronic monotone of his larynx-assist mechanism, and moral outrage showed in every seam and line of his weather-beaten face.

"Damn Michael to hell," he said. "And Walter Burnleigh with him if he's still top man. Toying with human life in the name of scientific expediency. You can blame Katherine if you wish, but they're the really guilty ones. I suppose next they'll be saying national security is at stake and we'll be listed as some sort of new secret weapon. Well, I've finally had enough of their awful injustice. I sat on the bench coping with human frailty and wrongdoing for close to twenty years, and by God, I don't intend to make mock of all that by doing nothing now. No matter what the risk. From now on, we must take a stand, and they must be stopped at any cost from what they're doing to us and will be doing to others who follow us."

For the first time Rachel wore a smile. It was the kind of fight she liked to hear. "Amen," she said.

John kept his thoughts to himself. The judge's

attitude was exemplary and understandable. He felt the same himself, and knew that out of charity as much as loyalty, he would support whatever the judge planned. But his mind told him that in the horrifying game of chess they played, any move they tried to make would be checked—and checked hard.

The judge, he thought, might have made the serious error of expecting the sort of justice he himself would mete out.

24

Henry Palmer had requested certain deep electrode implants into exceptionally delicate areas of the brain, and this required new and innovative surgical techniques. Michael felt he and Toni should first practice on a lifeless head to avoid possible mistakes with one of their ECs, and when Katherine got hold of him, he and Toni were in the autopsy room setting up. They had taken a male head from a container of formaldehyde and clamped it on the stainless-steel drainage table. There, it stared at them sightlessly from half-hooded eyes probably once blue but now turned by the preservative to a dull gray-yellow.

While Michael studied his notes and some X rays, Toni prepared the head.

Neither was aware of Katherine standing silently in the doorway. She watched while Toni quickly and expertly incised and laid back the scalp of the upper cranium and with an electric saw cut through the frontal bone, then diagonally back across the temporal fossa and around the lower parietal. She had lifted the bone free to expose the cortex, the wrinkled exterior layer of the brain, when Michael looked up. His eyes met Katherine's.

"Michael, I've got to talk to you."

"Now?" He gestured at the work he and Toni were doing. On seeing Katherine, he felt vague but immediate alarm. He was sure it had to do with Susan and the security problem she now posed. He was glad, in a way, she hadn't come with him to New York. Someone, unquestionably Katherine, had called the Plaza asking for Mrs. Burgess. Even though Burnleigh had told him to keep Susan happy, he had the feeling that was a trap of some kind and he didn't want the fact of a weekend with Susan to get back to the admiral, something he was certain Katherine was capable of making happen.

"I'm sorry. It's important. Toni, would you mind awfully?"

Toni rose from the autopsy table. "No problem. I can keep busy. Just call me." She went into the adjacent room with its electron microscope, closing the door behind her. The way she did made him wonder if she knew about Susan and him, too. He made a pretense of continuing work. "Well?"

Katherine saw he was uneasy and had no trouble guessing why. Friday night and Saturday she'd called Susan at home and there was no answer. Then she'd tried the Plaza Hotel in New York, and even though the operator had said there was no Mrs. Burgess registered, only Dr. Burgess, she was convinced Susan was with Michael. The rest of the weekend was then misery. In spite of everything she told herself about jealousy and every attempt to calm her raging emotions, her imagination had taken over. Seeing Michael and Susan together at dinner, at the theater, in bed, with the physical Michael driving Susan half-wild by making the kind of love he always had made to herself, had been a nightmare one movie after another hadn't erased.

She was almost glad she had bad news. Telling it to him was a kind of revenge. She came over to the autopsy table, made him wait a moment longer, then said, "We've got trouble brewing with the ECs."

"What kind of trouble?"

"They're on strike."

Michael put down a forceps and stared at her, half-laughing, half-incredulous. Katherine could see he was trying to take it in, to balance instinctive and immediate alarm with relief that she hadn't come to see him about Susan.

"The goddamned heads on strike? You've got to be kidding."

"I'm not. They refuse to cooperate further on any neurometric tests."

"Wait a minute. Whoa! Explain." Michael's incredulity grew.

Katherine shrugged. "The neurometric tests require verbal answers to questions. They refuse to speak."

"They refuse to speak," Michael repeated. "Just like that." His smile had disappeared. He stared at the lifeless head clamped to the table before him.

"They refuse to speak unless what?" He suddenly sounded petulant.

Katherine said, "Unless we give them guarantees to cut the work load in half."

Michael said slowly, "When did this nonsense start?"

"I don't know. Today, I guess."

"Where did they get the idea, from Flemming?"

"I don't think so. Not this time. I think it's Thurston."

"The judge? You're sure?"

"I think so."

"I'll be damned." Michael thought, then said, "Maybe he's just overtired. Who could substitute for him in Flemming's experiments?"

"Anybody, I suppose. Annette, Rachel. The new man when he comes up. Phillip. He'll be ready any day now."

"Anyone else?"

"We have those two women we did in March. The black and the gray-haired one. But neither is ready yet."

Michael frowned. "What does Flemming say to all of this?"

"The same as the others."

He rose. "Okay. Let's go talk to them." He went to the adjacent room, yanked the door open. "Toni, proceed without me. I'll be back in twenty minutes."

Katherine followed him silently through the operating area and then out the door across the corridor to the locker room to gear up in germ-protective clothing. There was a coldness in him she'd never seen before. It made her uneasy. Susan suddenly seemed unimportant.

She said, "Michael, don't get too tough with them. It could boomerang. Especially with Flemming. You know what he's like, and he's never forgiven you. If you have to bear down, let me do it with drugs or at least let me use drugs to get them all into an accepting frame of mind."

He didn't answer. Anxiety mounting, she followed him back across the corridor and into Ward Two.

25

When John told Susan what Thurston and the others planned, she had an immediate premonition of serious trouble.

"Michael will never agree to it, John. He's got his back to a wall. He has to produce results or else."

"I can't take away their right to protest, Susan. The most Michael can do is refuse."

She'd gone to her office to collect some data. When she returned, the duty nurse had left the control room, and glancing through the observation window, she saw him in the homeroom along with both Michael and Katherine.

Something told her not to go in. Perhaps it was just a sense of protocol, the mystique of medicine. What she saw had to do with doctors and medicine, and suddenly she was an outsider.

Thurston was talking.

Susan heard him say, "We cannot control or change the past but we will not lend ourselves to continuing this virtual slavery. Besides cutting back on our work time, we also insist on verifiable guarantees that you will accurately depict to all future ECs what is going to happen to them, not paint a deceptive picture of having a few more years of life and hiding the real future with nonsense like cerebral isolation and neurological blockage."

"I see," Michael said. His eyes met Helen's. "I gather you all concur with Judge Thurston."

She stared back at him in dignified defiance. "Indeed we do," she said quietly. "We also want to know where Peggy is now and where we are going ourselves when you're through with us."

Michael was thoughtful, then said, "Okay, I hear you. But I'm afraid that's all I do. First of all, I am not management, you are not a union. I am a doctor and you are experiments. You have been snatched from the grave and granted an incredible gift of further and useful life, one which might change the whole course of human history. But are you grateful? No. Instead, you moralize and quibble." He shrugged and went on, "I have no time for such nonsense. Nor does Borg-Harrison. This program has a schedule to fulfill, and the schedule does not allow me to have my hands tied."

He turned to Helen. "As for where you go when you leave here, I can only tell you it's a place where there is no more work and where all your physical needs will be beautifully taken care of."

It was too much for Rachel. "How about our psychological needs?" she demanded. "And I mean rest, reading, music, not another dose of tranquilizer from Katherine."

Katherine said coldly, "The only reason for your leaving here is death or insanity, so you'd hardly need the things you mention."

Michael nodded. "I agree. And now, suppose you all calm yourselves and get on with whatever you were supposed to be doing at this time."

Rachel's slender face contorted. "Look, you butcher bastards, didn't the judge make himself clear? No concessions, and you can go straight to hell."

Michael studied her, smiling slightly. Then he said, "So far, Rachel, you have contributed less to this program than almost anyone else. But I think I know a way to take care of that. I think I know a way to make you more than eager to work like crazy."

Even before he had turned away from Rachel, Susan finally saw what he was going to do. The realization hit her in the stomach with the force of a heavy punch. She couldn't breathe. She could only watch in overwhelming terror.

Without another word, Michael abruptly bent and flicked off the master power switch on Judge Thurston's console.

Thurston's mouth opened. He started to utter a protest. A kind of horror raged over his face.

Then went out.

His eyes stared, dulled. His lips slackened.

Seconds later, the muscles of his weather-beaten face sagged in immediate death.

It happened so quickly, no one reacted. Then the

nurse did. "Jesus, Doctor." He'd turned sheet-white. The fingers of one hand ran through his hair; his other hand went to his throat.

Katherine never moved. Her eyes went from Thurston to Michael and back to Thurston again. She was like a statue.

Susan tried to think. She reached for the control-room door. She had to get to John. Nothing else seemed to count.

His voice came unexpectedly sharp and clear over the audio. "No! Don't come in." He didn't use her name, but Susan knew he meant her. How did he know she was there? Was he just guessing? She could see him in the television monitor. He was without expression.

The others were different. Annette's eyes were closed as she prayed. Rachel's were shocked pinpoints of hate. Helen stared at Judge Thurston's dead face, disbelieving.

Michael addressed them. "Now," he said, "you should all have learned two things. One, I cannot be coerced. Two, you are all expendable. If you are still inclined to collective bargaining, I shall not hesitate to repeat what I have just done."

He turned to the nurse, his tone totally professional. He was the doctor again. He nodded at Thurston. "When you remove his scalp electrodes, replace them on Rachel. Any questions not answered by your electrode chart, just ask Miss McCullough. She's probably down in her office."

Katherine followed him to the germ lock. A faint smile had appeared on her lips.

When Susan heard the inner door open, she ducked into the other lock leading to John in the neurometric lab. But she didn't go in all the way. She couldn't face him. Or anyone. She stayed in the lock between the two doors and came back only when she was certain Michael and Katherine had left.

Going back out through the control room, she caught a last glimpse of Thurston. The nurse had covered him with a sheet of surgical gauze. There was just the lumpy white of the gauze, the sinister blue tube leading down from it, and below that, the heavy life-sustaining console, almost obscene in its anonymity.

She stripped off her germ-protective clothing and left it in a heap on the floor. She couldn't bear to see either Michael or Katherine, and they would still be in the locker room.

She went directly downstairs and home. She had to be alone to get herself under control. It was more important than any solace that she might give John and the others right now.

Taking a shower as though to wash away the horror of what she'd seen, she let a growing rage run through her, enjoying it, enjoying the sudden violent hatred for Michael that went with it. How was it possible that once, an eternity ago, she'd thought she loved him? She shuddered. Today, all she wanted to do was kill him. But she wouldn't. There was John, the others. Their lives, their safety, were more important.

When she finished her shower, she got dressed, went down to her car, and for an hour drove aimlessly around Washington. She'd always found she did her best thinking that way. She felt a terrible sense of urgency now; she could no longer afford to wait to act. If Michael could do the insane thing he'd just done to poor Thurston, he could as easily do the same to John. So she had to act, and act quickly, but she also had to act carefully. The anonymous warning she'd received wasn't a joke and it wasn't Katherine being jealous. It was real. She was, indeed, in danger.

Decisions began to formulate in her mind, first how to appear in Michael's and Katherine's eyes. When there was time for her to have heard the news, she'd tell Michael she knew. He'd be wary of her. She'd pretend suitable shock but she'd tell him she understood he'd been forced to do what he had, even sympathize. The EC program was more important than any one individual.

She'd use every feminine trick she could think of to make him believe her, because she had to keep things going with him. That was her only protection from Katherine, who would probably see through her. And if she had to go to bed with him again because it simply wasn't avoidable, she'd do that too. Other women had done more for the men they loved. You didn't die from sex.

As she drove home, she allowed herself briefly to relive the horror and think of Thurston. She didn't have to bother about avenging him. The rest of the world would take care of that. She only had to let the rest of the world know.

26

On first thought, Susan decided that the most logical place to seek help was the media. With an ever growing sense of paranoia, she was certain that anyone else she might contact, a state representative or senator, for example, would somehow, even inadvertently, alert Borg-Harrison. The Foundation was so prestigious it seemed almost all powerful.

She was well aware, however, that approaching any journalist could invite her immediate arrest by Federal authorities for breeching national security, if not for something far worse. It was all too easy to remember what had happened to Karen Silkwood. To say nothing of Judge Thurston. But time was of the essence. John couldn't last out forever, and she decided to try a major Washington newspaper. Although she wasn't very clear how any journalist could help without access to the Lab or some really concrete evidence as to what was going on there, she hoped at least to get some support and perhaps ideas about how to proceed to gather evidence.

The note in her typewriter had said her phone was tapped. It was the one part of it she found hard to believe, but she decided not to ignore it just the same. She went downtown shopping and used a public phone booth in a department store. Looking out through the booth's closed glass door, she could see no one watching her. Beginning to feel like a fool, she dialed the number she'd looked up earlier in her own phone book and told the operator who answered that she wanted to speak to an investigative reporter.

"City Desk."

"This is—" Her mind went blank. She couldn't give her own name—she hadn't thought of that. They could check up on her with Katherine or Michael or even Burnleigh and probably would. "—Mary Smith." She couldn't think of anything else.

The rest was just as bad. The reporter who picked up was an older man who pointedly called her Miss Smith and asked few questions, leaving her to do all the talking. By the time she was finished, she knew she had to sound like a disgruntled employee making up a fantastic story to get her boss in trouble. That, or totally crazy. Linking Borg-Harrison and Admiral Walter Burnleigh to secret brain experiments on disembodied but live human heads didn't have the slightest ring of truth or reality to it and telling the reporter she couldn't meet him because she was under surveillance or that he couldn't call her back because her phone was tapped made things even worse. If she'd felt a fool when she started, her embarrassment and frustration when she'd hung up were complete. She was close to tears.

She got no further on two more calls; the first to another newspaper, the second to one of the TV networks. But she collected condescending albeit good-humored advice from both similar to what she'd received from the reporter. "Get us concrete evidence—photographs, documents, anything you can find—and we'll take it from there."

It was what she'd been prepared for them to say all along and she kicked herself for not having done so in the first place. How to get such evidence was another matter.

She knew nothing about cameras and would have to buy one—and surely that would attract attention. Besides, the goldfish-bowl existence of the ECs made taking secret pictures almost impossible.

A few inches of one of the many monitoring videotapes of the ECs would be easy to conceal, but there was a hitch there, also. The cabinets they were kept in required two different keys. The duty nurse was in charge of one; the other was kept by the chief security officer.

That left documentation, something in writing. She decided on a thorough search of offices; Michael's, Katherine's, even Toni's or Al Luczynski's might turn up something she could use and which she could smuggle out in the regular office mail. And it crossed her mind that she might stumble onto something with which to lure Al Luczynski into helping.

Who knew what, but it was quite clear he had an almost consuming interest in her.

She waited until Friday night, when no one ever stayed late, and begged off from dinner and a Kennedy Center ballet with Michael. Her excuse was work.

He didn't make it easy. "Can't you do whatever it is tomorrow?"

"I wish I could."

He'd looked dubious.

So had Katherine at six o'clock when, passing by, she'd stopped to say good night. "You work too hard, Susan." Susan tried to see some sign in her face that Katherine was aware she knew what Michael had done to Thurston. But Katherine's pleasant smile was inscrutable. It made her seem more of a menace than ever.

Around nine o'clock, the last researcher left and a night security guard came by on his first hourly check. He was a friendly older man who usually regaled her with baseball scores.

"Staying late again, miss?"

"Yes, I am."

"If I'm not at my desk when you leave, I'll be in the cafeteria. Just ring the desk buzzer and I'll come right down to check you out."

Susan said she would, waited for five minutes after he'd disappeared, then took the elevator downstairs and went directly to Michael's office.

Gladys's secretarial area was in darkness and her typewriter shrouded. Both Michael's and Katherine's doors were shut. Going to Michael's, she nearly panicked. Suppose he was still there? She got herself under control and went in. The office was empty. She turned on lights, looked around, and decided his desk was the best place to begin. It was unlocked, which meant there was probably nothing there, but she decided to look anyway.

Be obvious, she thought. If anyone comes, don't look guilty. Make a show of belonging. Say Michael asked for a simulation on a patient death due to infection and has left notes for you to pick up. And if it's Michael himself, say you're looking for some data you gave him.

No one came through the door.

And she found nothing. Neither in his desk nor in his file case—also unlocked—and not among the many medical books and papers which filled his bookshelves. There were no photographs or X rays, no tapes of any kind. She didn't even come across any case histories of ECs or records of severance operations.

She went to Katherine's office. Being there somehow frightened her more than being in Michael's, and she went very quickly through Katherine's desk drawers and her file case. Once again she came up empty-handed. She pulled out some folders stacked on Katherine's shelves. One contained notes on schizophrenia as related to economic standing. In another there was a series of case histories of various types of insanity, a score or more of them. None was identified, but Susan had a numbing suspicion of who they were.

In a last folder she found a half-dozen memoranda

on ECs of several years ago, but nothing to show they were anything but normal people. They were classified without names, just numbers and as cases sixteen through twenty-one. Susan found even thinking of them painful. It was too easy to forget that the EC program had been in existence for so long. That it was not confined to just Peggy, Annette, and Thurston, and to Helen and Rachel. Or to John.

The tumbril brought you, the executioner waited, the crowd roared. You mounted the scaffold, the priest prayed. With a rush, the blade fell.

Darkness.

Except there wouldn't be any tumbril or crowds or priest or executioner. There'd be surgeons. And instead of the rattle of the guillotine, there would be the hiss of anesthesia and the surgeon's silent razor-sharp scalpel.

And instead of the damp, dark, forever-silent peace of the eternal grave, would come the relentless electric hum of the console motors echoing in your skull, and in your eardrums the unceasing liquid gurgle of the pharyngostomy drain.

She'd just started to put the case folders back and was wondering where to look next, when there was a faint sound behind her.

She froze.

One second, two. Her mind registered clothes, a body moving silently and close.

She tried to turn, couldn't. Her resolution to be brazen failed. Her hands, fixed to the folders, were miles away and didn't belong to her.

Until someone else's hand touched her shoulder.

She stifled a scream.

Katherine's voice said, "All right, Susan, perhaps you'd like to explain what you are doing in my office."

Susan turned slowly to face her.

27

It wasn't Katherine. It was Al Luczynski. He stood big and bearish in the middle of the office, hands shoved casually into the pockets of his white medical coat, wearing a wide grin. He smelled strongly of antiseptic. "Scared the hell out of you, didn't I?"

He said it in Katherine's cool voice and laughed.

Susan managed a weak smile back. Al's mimicry slowly fell into place, and her terror receded.

"What on earth are you doing here so late?" he asked. His eyes were friendly and without suspicion.

Susan found her voice. "Katherine asked me to run up a computer simulation on a death due to infection. She said she left some notes on her desk, and I can't find them." She tried to think of something else to say. "You must have the weekend watch." She began to sidle for the door.

He followed. "Such was my good fortune," he said. He glanced at his watch. "I'm taking a break, can I buy you a coffee?" He grinned again, this time hugely, enjoying his joke. Coffee in the cafeteria was free for staff.

Perhaps because of his grin and the hopefulness in his bearded face, Susan suddenly saw a chance. There had to be records somewhere—surely in the surgical area, where her card still denied her access.

"Sure," she said. "I'd love it."

His surprised look of pleasure buoyed her confidence. As they made their way to the cafeteria, she very carefully began to flirt, asking him questions about his work, his home, where he came from, what his dreams in life were.

Halfway through coffee, she knew it was now or never.

"Al, I need a drug."

"One of those, are you? Mainline or otherwise?"

She laughed appropriately and put her hand over his. "Be serious. It's not for me. It's for one of my experiments. Michael said he'd let me have some but he forgot, and now he's off for the weekend. So is Katherine, and there's none in the control room. The nurse said I'd have to try the drug cabinet in surgery."

"Why not?" he said. "What kind?"

"Phenmetrazine."

"Phenmetrazine? That would be pretty hot stuff to an EC. You know that, don't you? Too much and his brain will go up in smoke."

She nodded. "I understand that. I'd be very careful with it."

He studied her, then smiled suddenly. "Okay. So long as you're aware."

"Thanks, Al."

She summoned up her courage again. The worst that could happen was he'd say no to her next request and she'd only get the drug. At least she'd make John happy.

She softened her voice, smiled gently at him, and left her hand on his, blatantly touching one of his fingers with hers in a kind of silent caress. "Would you take me?"

"To surgery?"

"I know I don't have clearance, but I'm dying of curiosity, Al. It's like the secret tower room in a movie."

"Gosh, Susan, I'm not sure."

"No one would have to know."

"What about the nurses?"

"They'll all presume I've been cleared. They'd never think otherwise. Please."

He surrendered. "Okay, why not! But I must be nuts." He laughed pointedly. "Or in love. And dammit, you ever tell Michael or anyone else, I'll put your head on a console." He made a ferocious face and drew his finger across his neck. "Got it? Promise?"

"Promise."

They finished their coffee. She couldn't believe how easy it had been. Leaving, she saw the elder security guard with two others at a corner table, playing their usual game of poker.

Moments later, she found herself in the elevator going up one flight. When the doors opened, she stepped into the now familiar hall of the third floor.

But instead of entering the locker room to gear up in a germ-protective hood and clothing as she always did, Susan found herself at the door to Ward One.

Luczynski produced his identity card, slotted it, and they went in. Susan quickly registered what lay before her. They had entered a small lobby with hospital flooring and bare walls. Here and there were trolleys of medical equipment; behind a nurse's station was a wall of intensive-care monitors, their illuminated faces creating ever-moving patterns of green and red light. There were TV monitors, too, a half-dozen of them. On three, Susan saw the unmistakable images of heads held motionless by curved surgical steel tongs, three ECs she hadn't known of. Who were they and where were they?

A nurse was at the desk, writing. She had looked up when they entered, then back down, ignoring them.

Luczynski said, "This way," and Susan followed again, now into a short corridor. To her left, double doors wide enough to admit a stretcher-bed gave onto an operating room. Luczynski stopped by a big steel cabinet, opened it. Inside were shelves of drugs. He peered. One of his big fingers probed about. "Phenmetrazine ... let's see now. Probably down here. How much do you need?"

Susan guessed. "About seventy-five milligrams a day for a couple of weeks." She held her breath. Had she grossly misstated the amount?

"It comes in tablet form, if I remember correctly," he said. He produced a bottle. "Here we are. Twenty-five milligrams each. You'll need to liquefy them.

Make a solution of fifty milligrams to a milliliter of sterile water."

Susan took the bottle. "Thanks, Al." She rewarded him with a kiss on his bearded cheek.

He laughed, hugged her shoulder. "Jackpot! You just won the full tour."

He showed her the operating room. She was dazzled. She had never seen such an array of equipment and she almost forgot where she was until she saw the silent life-sustaining console with its two vertical stainless-steel poles to which surgical tongs would be attached. They looked to Susan like the uprights of a guillotine. Draped over the console was a long blue rubber-nylon tube and coils of smaller tubes and wires all waiting to be attached somewhere up inside the raw stump of neck. Behind was a row of vital-signs monitors, their inactive screens now dark.

A chill ran through her whole body, like the shadow of death. It was all waiting, soon to be occupied and used by someone not yet an EC. Someone who was still whole and had yet to face the soul-destroying horror of only half-being.

As though reading her mind, Luczynski said, "The next occupant came in just two hours ago from a hospital. Want to see her?"

Susan nodded numbly and went with him into a pre-op room next door.

There was a nurse there, bent over a bed giving someone an injection. When she straightened, Susan saw the woman, her freshly shaved head framed by the white pillow and looking small and delicate and terribly vulnerable. She had the almost child-like face of someone quite young, and her gray eyes had the blank stare of the heavily drugged. Around the base of her neck they'd already painted a thin red incision line with small numbers scattered here and there above and below it.

Nausea. Instant waves of it. Terror.

Run. Leave the wing, the building. Forever. Why was she even here? She forced herself to concentrate. Think. Remember.

And heard the nurse say, "Doctor, I'm not happy with my ECG readings. Could you take a look?"

Luczynski turned to Susan, frowning slightly, suddenly alert. "Maybe you ought to go back now, okay? I may be in for trouble. I'll catch you later."

"Of course." She slipped away, glancing back only once to see him already bending over the bed.

In the lobby the nurse was still on station, the monitors behind her a lacework of color. She turned from a TV screen with its image of some unknown EC, and half-raised a hand in greeting. Susan gestured "hello" in return. The nurse went back to the monitor.

And Susan remembered with a jolt why she'd come. She'd wanted evidence of what was going on here, and she'd seen nothing in the operating-room area she could use. Somewhere there had to be files, records, X rays. And who were those other ECs, where were they?

There was only one other door off the lobby. It had to lead to them. And perhaps to something she could use. Looking back, she saw the nurse still watching the TV screen. Above her a wall clock said it was five past ten. She probably had a few minutes before Luczynski would finish whatever he had to with the young woman and come looking for her downstairs. If he caught her still here, she could always claim she'd gone the wrong way, bluff it somehow. He couldn't say much—he'd let her up here when he wasn't supposed to.

She quickly opened the door and stepped into a silent, half-dark corridor beyond. The air was cool. She saw no one. She closed the door softly behind her and started forward cautiously, taking her first step into a nightmare.

28

_____

Overheads in the corridor had been dimmed and most of the light that made rectangular patterns against the darkness of floor and walls seemed to come from windows in the rooms beyond or through open doors.

Something in Susan told her to proceed no further, some nameless rising fear. She made herself go to the first window.

It gave onto a small isolation room, almost just a booth, but big enough for the EC who occupied it, a balding middle-aged male whose eyes looked blankly at nothing. It was a familiar scene, a once active human being held a rigid prisoner over a life-sustaining mass of complex machinery. So close to someone in that condition who was a stranger, Susan felt something of the same shock she'd felt when first seeing John, and realized how accustomed she'd become to him and the others in the homeroom.

Without protective clothing, she couldn't go in.

She flicked switches on a two-way speaker control panel by the door. Immediately there was the familiar electric hum of the heavy life-sustaining console and the gurgle of the pharyngostomy tube.

Susan said, "Hello. Care for a visitor?"

The eyes blinked to life. The man's tongue flicked at a tiny switch suspended by his lips. His voice, like the voices of all ECs, came to her in a slightly electronic monotone.

"Who are you?"

"I'm Susan. I'm a new nurse doing orientation."

"I'm Phillip. I'm thirty-eight. I've been an EC for five months. I was a teacher." It was virtually a recital.

"What do they have you doing, Phillip?"

"Brain work. Experiments. See how much I can learn in a day when they tickle the right places." For a second a flash of pride lit his eyes. "I've been learning Chinese. Mandarin has something like forty thousand logographic characters, you know. I memorized six hundred of them in less than a week. And I've done a whole course in intermediate physics since I came out of prelim."

"Why did you volunteer?"

"I was going to die, I think. They told me I was."

"Do you think you would have?"

He didn't answer. A veil seemed to drop behind his eyes, protectively curtaining his mind from her.

Susan tried a different approach; she wanted to keep him talking. "Do you ever see the others?"

"Others? You mean Anne-Marie and Alice?"

Susan realized he thought they were the only ones.

"Yes," she said. "Tell me about them."

He smiled for the first time. He said, "They let me see them once a week. We're all wheeled into a special room and left facing each other so we can talk. They're about two months behind me. Alice was a physicist. She's helped me with my course. Anne-Marie was a lawyer. They're both still in prelim."

"Where is this prelim you keep mentioning?"

He looked surprised at the question. "It's not a place. Prelim stands for preliminary. It just means they haven't started experimental work yet. At least Anne-Marie hasn't."

"Why not?"

He didn't answer. A curtain came down again behind his eyes.

"Please tell me," Susan said.

He hesitated, then seemed to decide to trust her. "When this first happens," he said, "you're not yourself for a long while, so no one is allowed to see you. Just doctors and some special nurses. I couldn't speak for weeks. All I wanted was to be dead."

"But they saved you. They gave you a new life," Susan argued.

She wanted to provoke him, and succeeded. A sneer twisted his features. "Do you think so?"

"Don't you?"

"I've accepted it. Alice has accepted it. But Anne-Marie still won't. She had an accident and claims she was recovering. She keeps saying they murdered her and she won't ever cooperate."

"And did they?"

His eyes showed sudden fear. "No . . . no, of course not. I would never think that. Never. They're kind and good. They saved my life. You said so yourself."

It was a litany. And a lie. Susan knew he saw her as part of the team that had betrayed a promise. The gulf between them made further questions a waste of time. She avoided his stare and glanced at her watch. She'd already used up too much precious time. She held down rising panic and prayed Al Luczynski would take longer than she thought he would.

"I've got to go," she said.

"Sure."

His eyes clouded once more as he retreated into his mind.

Susan turned off the two-way speaker system and headed down the corridor for the next rectangle of light. There were two windows, side by side. The rooms beyond were occupied by ECs, the first a middle-aged woman with gray hair shaved in several patches to admit deep electrodes. She seemed to be asleep. In the second room there was a strikingly beautiful young black woman whose shaven head was bare of any electrodes and glistened darkly in the soft light. Susan guessed at once that this was Anne-Marie. Her eyes, staring dully and straight ahead as Phillip's had, suddenly flared on seeing Susan and suffused immediately with such burning hatred that Susan instinctively stepped backward.

Then she turned on the speaker system. "You're Anne-Marie."

The woman's answering voice rose at once through its electronic assist. It was almost a snarl.

"Was Anne-Marie, you goddamned murderess. Was."

Susan left her. Further on, there was a small dispensary, its door open and plunged in darkness. She flicked on lights, saw only medical equipment; extra monitors and surgical trays. Beyond, in what she guessed was a nurses' common room, there were deep chairs, a couch, a low table, and books. Across from it was a storeroom containing various mobile video equipment, cameras, and other recording apparatus. In a third room Susan saw vital-signs monitors and power cable outlets and guessed it was probably used for the EC meetings Phillip had talked about.

Then she found herself at the corridor's end, with only one more door to open.

Above it was a red light. Was it just a fire stair? She nearly turned back, but some strange intuition made her stay. She had seen what must be everything Ward One had to offer. Except for one thing, and it lurked in her mind, an indefinable terror which had begun to creep up her spine to the back of her neck and into her mind to completely control her.

She knew what lay beyond the door and had to go in there.

And yet couldn't bring herself to move. Her hand

rested on the doorknob, frozen to it, motionless. Until with an almost violent motion she turned it.

The door swung inward, thudded shut behind her. She found herself not on a fire escape but in another corridor, a very short one almost like a germ lock. Before her, red lettering on a second door said, "Disposal Unit."

She moved automatically now, robotlike, caution forgotten. The door was heavy but gave with muffled ease.

There were no more corridors beyond it, no more doors. Just a room. A room and the familiar medicinal smell, the familiar cool air, the familiar hum of electric motors.

But no twilight here. Instead, the glare of unshielded overheads. Assaulting cold light and a strange sound, a noise like lapping water and falling leaves together.

Her eyes adjusted slowly, and she saw. Something rose in her throat. A protest at sheer horror. And died. She wanted to turn and run. Couldn't. Her legs were lead.

Heads. Rows of them. Hair unkempt and white above insane faces grown old with rapid age. Eyes that darted wildly like those of trapped animals, or stared mindlessly into their own nightmares. Faces that snarled and mocked and twisted into shrieking laughter.

But silently.

No babbling whispers here. No wild cries. No chilling screams. No gibbering obscenities. Each alone in his own private hell, silent save for the fluttering liquid noises made by frantic lips and tongues.

A silence guaranteed forever, witnessed only in the untraceable files on madness locked away in Katherine's office. A ragged scar down the throat of each, mute evidence that their larynxes had been removed.

Susan stood motionless. How many? A score? At least. Medical experiments kept alive until death came, with no one accused of causing it. Passive subjects on whom, undoubtedly, every new drug that came along was tried.

The face of a young woman pleaded. Was it Peggy? Yes. Susan gently touched her head.

"Don't give up. We'll get you back before you know it."

A glimmer of hope flared. Then the eyes dulled, shifted away. Peggy had heard yet one more lie.

But Susan didn't see. Her attention had gone elsewhere. Behind the rows of heads.

Along one wall there were metal shelves and on them a dozen glass containers. And in each container, floating suspended in formaldehyde, one of the "disposed," waiting for the autopsy room.

Staring half-open eyes had turned from brown or blue or green or gray to a dull yellow. Decomposed skin and wrinkled lips were slack with death long forgotten. Colorless hair floated motionless in the tissue-clouded liquid. White tendrils of preserved flesh hung in ragged tails from truncated necks.

Two were without eyes. Three were children.

A terrible iron vise gripped Susan's chest. Her

breath stopped. The room darkened, receded, the rows of heads seemed far, far away suddenly. She knew she was going to faint and found strength to move.

She turned to flee, to hide forever from all of it, to blot it out, to forget.

And stopped.

Someone stood in the doorway, not a nurse. Not Al Luczynski this time, imitating Katherine.

This time it was Katherine herself.

Her face, the expression in her eyes, was ice.

29

Time stood still. The watery fluttering silenced as though even the mindless could be cowed.

Katherine smiled frigidly and said, "I don't know how you got here or what you're up to—Luczynski is probably responsible, and if he is, God help him. Whatever, I shall have to discuss this with Admiral Burnleigh and see what he wants to do with you. Meanwhile, I'd like to remind you of the security oath you signed when you first came. The government has ways of dealing with people who ignore it."

She disappeared as silently as she had come, leaving Susan once more to the renewed sound of the living dead. When she finally regained the corridor outside the disposal room, Katherine was nowhere to be seen.

She made her way out of Ward One. The nurse at the nurse's station was still occupied and didn't look up. She went downstairs to her office, methodically tidied her desk, and left for home. She saw no one except the security guard, who had left the cafeteria poker game and was back at his post by the exit to the outer main lobby. He was his usual friendly self, but Susan knew Katherine had to be the reason he was no longer upstairs.

When she got home, the phone was ringing. It could only be Michael. She waited until it stopped, then took the receiver off the hook. She couldn't face thinking any more of him, or of tomorrow, what they might do to her and if she would ever see John again.

She took a sleeping pill and fell into troubled sleep. Toward dawn she had a terrible dream. Her family's old farm dog appeared as just a head, jerking in bloody spasms about the dust of the dirt road that ran by their house and yapping angrily. John was there, his once gangling self. "Don't be frightened, Susan," he said. "We'll get a console from Admiral Burnleigh." He wandered off and Michael appeared, dressed in surgical clothes. "We've got to stop him from barking, Susan. He's no good as an experiment the way he is." He pushed her to one side and, ignoring her pleas, cut the dog's tongue out. Then its gargled screams became her own and it was herself, not the dog, who writhed in the dust. She awoke, sitting up, hands to her throat, her body drenched in sweat.

The sky was just lightening, and she sat a long time by her window staring at the silent street below. Her dream hung on, finally displaced only when she began to be haunted by the pale face of the young woman in the pre-op bed. In just another hour or so she would be severed from her body.

Susan took a shower and had coffee and tried to erase the memory and couldn't. Fear sat in her like a stone, but she had to get to the lab and try to see John, no matter what. Yesterday, she had still hoped to protect him from anxiety and danger. But time had run out and she'd accomplished nothing except probably to put him in even greater jeopardy. Now, if she were to protect him at all, and herself as well, she was going to have to tell him everything. She would need all his intelligence and insight.

When she arrived at the lab and walked down the awakening office corridor, she felt almost nauseated with the expectation that at any next step she'd be stopped and then God only knew what—arrested, taken away, locked up, perhaps. To her surprise, nothing happened. Gladys peered over her rhinestone harlequin glasses and waved bony ringed fingers in greeting; Toni Soong, slim and crisp in her white doctor's smock, whipped by with a hurried, "Hi, Susan"; Palmer said his usual "Good morning, dear child," before burying himself again in the mass of papers that was his usual morning desktop.

Could Katherine not have told them? And if not, then why not? Susan couldn't find an answer, and it made the very normality of everything seem even more ominous.

There was no sign anywhere of Al Luczynski, so she knocked at his office door. When no one answered, she pushed the door open.

He was at his desk, doing paperwork.

"Al. Hi. We've got to talk."

"Later maybe, Susan. I'm busy right now." His mouth smiled but his eyes didn't.

Susan persisted. "About last night. Honestly, I didn't mean to cause trouble."

"No problem."

"But Katherine must have said something."

He shrugged and didn't answer, which told Susan more than if he had. She guessed Katherine had been really vile to him.

"I'm sorry, Al, really. Maybe when you're not so busy." She retreated, closing the door gently behind her and knowing he'd probably never tell her what had happened.

She went to her own office in the research section and pretended to work. The morning crawled. She wasn't due to visit John until early afternoon and she didn't dare now get caught seeing him off-schedule. Midmorning coffee break came. It was the time Michael usually stopped by to visit, and she almost expected him to, until she remembered the operation. She tried hard to push it out of her mind, to keep last night's nightmare from coming back.

When he telephoned, it caught her so by surprise, that her first words were, "You're supposed to be operating."

"I am. I took a break."

All she could remember after that was listening speechless to his telling her they would have dinner at Annapolis. Without waiting for her to speak, he reminded her of a report she'd promised, then abruptly hung up.

When she'd put her own receiver back, she stared a long while at the phone. Could Katherine have failed to tell him?

She skipped lunch in the cafeteria. Katherine always went there. Instead, she talked a lab technician into making up half a dozen vials of liquid phenmetrazine, using some of the tablets from the bottle Al Luczynski had given her.

At two o'clock she took the elevator to the third floor, changed into protective gear in the locker room, and joined John in the computer-crammed surroundings of his special lab. They had worked for half an hour and she was just on the verge of finally speaking out when, as though reading her mind, he suddenly said, "You're hiding something, Susan. Something painful to me, I imagine, otherwise you would have let me know. Shall I guess? You've found where the elephants go to die."

She told him then, the whole story, from her attempt to enlist media help to how she'd used Al Luczynski to gain access to Ward One, and how Katherine had caught her in the disposal room. And finally said, "Oh, God, John, I didn't want to burden you, but it's going to take both of us. What are we going to do?"

His answer was casual, infuriatingly so. She couldn't believe it. He even smiled. "Do? Simple. We're going to do what we should have done long ago—figure some way to get you permanently lost."

"No."

His smile faded and his hollow eyes became intensely serious. "Not no, Susan. Yes. You've stepped over the line. The danger you present to them now might outweigh their need for you. Two of us dead won't do either of us any good. Be realistic—you have a lifetime ahead of you, while it might only be six months before I go.".

He waited until he seemed to think his warning had sunk in, and then became all business. "Okay, now to practicalities. You'll have to move fast, catch them off guard. There must be money from what we put together to buy the house to last you a good while. Dump your tail—country roads are usually easiest, I imagine, perhaps around my mother's home, where you know them and they don't. Then, New York, take any standby seat to Europe, preferably to Sweden, which might grant you political asylum, and don't come back until this crowd is convinced you never intend to blow a whistle."

Susan kept her temper but was pointedly firm. "Forget it, John, same answer as before. I'm not walking out on you. Not ever."

He looked genuinely taken aback. "Nonsense."

"No. It's not nonsense. You know I could never leave you and live with myself."

He stared at her for a long moment. It was the same sort of stare he always had given her when she'd dug in her heels and stood up for her rights; calculating how much she really meant what she said and how far he could go with heavy persuasion.

She repeated herself. "I'm not leaving. And that's that."

It was a familiar look. She wasn't about to give an inch.

John's eyes narrowed; then he retreated. He said slowly, "We'll see about it. Did you bring me some pick-me-up?"

"Yes." She took a vial of phenmetrazine from her pocket.

"Let's have a shot. A hundred milligrams' worth will do me just fine, thank you."

Susan stripped the metal seal from the vial and upended it into the drug receptor of John's console. "You start with fifty," she said firmly. She pushed the required button on the receptacle command system. A recessed needle pierced the vial's rubber stopper and drained out the precise amount she ordered.

John reacted quickly. "Interesting," he said. "Being without a body, the stuff gets to you right away."

"How long should it last?"

"Don't know. A couple of hours, probably. We'll see." He winked and said, "Okay, that's neurometrics for today. We have bigger fish to fry, and I'm going to need your help."

He sucked his sip-puff tube between his lips, activated his terminal. Green words flowed across the gray of the terminal's screen.

"Memory bank request."

"Access granted."

"Reveal disc eight-four."

"Eight-four available."

"Reveal level ninety-seven."

"Ninety-seven available."

Susan said, "At the risk of being too forward, do you mind filling me in?"

John interrupted his program and told her what he was doing. "I've put everything I know about the whole Borg-Harrison brain-research program," he said, "into a memorandum and filed it in Mainframe's memory. Its reference number is 19479B. Once I find the encoded password which hooks us into the national network of computer nodes, all I have to do is tell Mainframe to transmit the file. The whole country will know what goes on here in seconds."

Susan felt herself flush half with anger, half with chagrin. So, all the time she'd been going half-crazy trying to find an escape solution on her own, he'd been doing the same thing, and probably with a much greater chance of success.

"Thanks," she said tartly. "Thanks for telling me."

"Ah? Irritation? What about your sneaking about? I suppose you told me?"

"I intended to, but I'm not talking about that," she lied, "I'm talking about the phenmetrazine. If I'd known, I never would have gotten the damned stuff for you."

"You weren't talking about the drug," John said, "and you know it. But let's forget it. And don't get angry, it will get neither of us anywhere. Besides, there's no jug of wine around to pour on me when you find your inferior brain has rendered you speechless."

It defused Susan. She laughed in spite of herself

and touched her gloved hand to his forehead. "You're incorrigible. The original male chauvinist. Can't you understand?" she said. "You'll kill yourself. You'll never live to see it happen."

"If I sleep," he shot back, "I'm not likely to see it happen either. Try to understand that perhaps I place a slightly different value on life than you now, so enough is enough, run up some EEG stuff as cover for me. We need to look as though we were working."

He readdressed his terminal. "Extent numbers are three?"

"Correct."

"Please reveal."

"Sorry. Password?"

He cursed and began to feed the terminal a permutation formula designed to second-guess the wanted number and force its revelation.

Susan watched him. He looked drawn, exhausted, five years older than he had looked last week. His hair, which they'd let grow, was thin and lank. Surely the doctors must have noticed. Noticed and chalked it up to increased pressure to produce results with his AAD theory. They didn't give a damn if he burned himself out, as long as he came up in time with the right solution to their program. Flemming? Oh, we got what we needed before we sent him to Disposal.

Studying his sensitive face, she thought of that awful hell she'd seen last night, which had to lie ahead for John, his lips forever silent and his brilliant mind tortured and alone. And she thought of

John as she had dreamed of him, the way he'd once been, tall, gangling, his walk a sneakered lope. And remembered John, too, in his baggy boxer shorts and T-shirt pretending to pick at Percival's fleas.

What had happened to them both? They had been so innocent, so loving, so happy, and so trusting of life. And now John was a helpless non-person living in hell and she was a kind of slave forced to watch him die right before her eyes.

She felt an anger she'd never before known, a helpless inner raging at injustice. She turned away from him, and switching on her EEG computer and terminal, began feeding what she read of Rachel's brain waves into the program she'd written the day before. Whatever fell on the heads of Michael and Katherine and Burnleigh, too, if John succeeded, was what they deserved.

An hour later, a nurse came in to dispense calmative drugs and to announce rest period. She uncapped a vial of Thorazine, administered five cc's to John. He grinned at her. "Do your damnedest, lady." And winked at Susan when the nurse went into the other room.

"I'll have more of ours, please."

"John, no."

"Right now."

Susan saw sudden frenzy in his eyes and stopped protesting. Arguing might do him more harm than the drug, but she determined to cheat in the future and always give him less than whatever he asked for. He couldn't see the computer command on the drug receptacle; she could. She administered the phenmetrazine and filled out her scheduled time with him by running up computer programs to cover what John was doing. It took everything she had even to pretend to work, and two hours later, when she left, she felt depressed almost to the point of despair.

John barely registered her absence. Funny thing with drugs, he thought. With no body to absorb them, he could literally feel them doing their different jobs—calming, stimulating, warring against each other—so acutely sensitized had his brain become. He felt the phenmetrazine winning. But would it outlast the Thorazine? He would soon know.

He began to think of Susan. He hadn't had the heart to tell her his real fears, nor that they were all for her. If he didn't soon produce solid results with his alternate-area-development work, he'd burn out the way all ECs did, and Susan would take his place on his console. If he did succeed, she'd take his place anyway. She knew too much for them ever to take the chance of letting her go free.

It worried him that she'd said nobody seemed to know she'd discovered the disposal room. It had to mean Katherine had something up her sleeve and would probably move quickly with it. In turn, that meant he would have to redouble his efforts.

Death pretended devotion to science and humanitarianism and wore a hood and a surgical gown and carried a scalpel.

Death laid a gloved finger on a switch. Just one flick and you were not. You'd cease to be.

That's all it took.

That or a last wheeled ride to join the others who'd gone before you to the disposal room. You didn't have a choice. Your fate was left to your jailers.

30

The maître d'hôtel at the exclusive Rive Droite off L Street, midway between the White House and Dupont Circle, had welcomed almost every beautiful couple imaginable into the restaurant's rarefied candlelit atmosphere. He rated among the best the couple who'd reserved for eight-thirty, and with his experienced eye marked them as professional people, lawyers or doctors.

The woman, who was quite beautiful, wore a straight black off-the-shoulder twenties-style silk dress and expensive jewelry—small diamond earrings set in a cluster of emeralds, a diamond-and-emerald pendant perfectly suited to her slender neck and titian hair, caught up for the evening in a classic French chignon. On one arm she displayed a heavy gold cuff that matched the unusual amber color of her eyes and the lightly tanned complexion of her perfectly made-up face.

Escorting her to the table, the maître d' also no-

ticed the seductive fragrance of her very expensive
perfume. It was Joy by Patou. She would be quite
irresistible to most men, he thought.

Her companion, in a dark gray suit immaculately
tailored to his tall athletic build, had a well-bred air
and intelligent eyes and something else, too—the
kind of self-confident expression which sometimes
borders on ruthlessness.

Lawyers, the maître d' decided incorrectly while
seating them at their table. And watch out for her.
She was a woman who usually got what she wanted.

He gave them menus, signaled their waiter and
the sommelier, then forgot them as he went to greet
another couple.

Katherine pretended to study the menu. She knew
Michael was nervous and more than curious as to
why she'd insisted so urgently at the last moment
that he take her to dinner. She'd phoned at four
o'clock from outside the office.

"What's up?"

"What's up is that we're dining together."

"Oh? When?"

"Tonight."

"Tonight?" His laugh hadn't hidden his obvious
annoyance. "You must be kidding. That's impossible."

"Then make it possible. This is important. I've
already phoned the Rive Droite for reservations. You
can pick me up around eight. I'll give you a drink
before we go."

"Now, wait a minute, Katherine. I have other
plans."

"Change them." She'd hung up abruptly and had been dressed and confidently waiting for him, ice in the cooler on the living-room sideboard, when he rang her doorbell.

She kept conversation to small talk and shop as they drove to the restaurant. She was in no hurry to fill him in on what she really wanted to say. Taking her time and making him wait was part of softening him up for it. So were the two hours she'd spent on her makeup, selecting and putting on the dress she'd bought at Bergdorf's on her last trip to New York, and the right earrings and pendant from jewelry her father had given her. She planned to use every weapon her sex had bestowed on her.

The exterior calm she displayed wasn't quite matched by what she felt inside, however. She was about to take a calculated risk, and although she was pretty sure her chances to succeed were excellent, there was always the odd chance she'd fail. If she'd learned nothing else in psychiatry, it was that people were too unpredictable for rules to apply. Studying Michael in the candlelight, she allowed herself the briefest secret surrender to her mixed emotions. She wanted him, and wanted him badly. She always had. And she wanted him for herself alone. That would not change. At the same time she had to protect herself and her own goals.

She ordered, chatted airily, was casually affectionate, and waited for him to make the first move. She didn't think it would be long. She counted on his impatience; Michael had never been able to stand not knowing.

She was right. He lasted only until the entrée.

"Okay, Katherine, you've got me here, you've managed to look your most seductive, so let's dispense with the preliminaries. What's it all about?"

She was prepared. She had carefully rehearsed every possible scenario. "All right. Suppose we start with Susan."

His slightly wary smile relaxed. It was a question he'd obviously expected. He shrugged. "So, I've been seeing quite a bit of her."

Katherine smiled. "Twenty hours out of every twenty-four, I'd say."

"If you insist."

"I don't." She put a hand gently over one of his, kept her voice soft. "Relax, Michael. I'm not going to play the rejected woman. I really don't give a damn if you're sleeping with her or not, for whatever she might be worth. What you and I have had for five years is too important to lose over your little extracurricular affair, whether it's just a passing fancy or not. I never made a demand of exclusivity. I always felt what we had together was more important than raw sex." She smiled again. "And I have to confess, I haven't exactly been blameless all these years either. So don't feel too guilty."

She studied him then from behind half-lowered eyelids, enjoying the flicker of hurt he wasn't able to hide. Michael's brand of arrogance, she thought, wouldn't accept her getting into bed with any man but himself. Or that any other man might be a better lover.

She assumed a practical tone. "I'm more concerned with our Miss McCullough's working role. And," she added, "yours."

Wariness returned to his eyes. "Go on," he said.

"Susan has become too close to Flemming for my liking. I should think for yours, too. She spends more time with him than she does in her office. I can't believe it's all dedication to work."

His laugh was genuine. "And? Am I supposed to be jealous or what?"

"Hardly jealous, Michael, but suspicious, yes. Has it never occurred to you that your little maneuver with the judge might have inspired in Flemming exactly the opposite from what you hoped? Rebellion instead of abject surrender? It would be far more in keeping with his character. As for Susan, have you never thought that she might actually see you as a murderer and that all the sweet nothings she must whisper every night in your ear might be calculated to keep your guard down while she and her pet head scheme to turn you in?"

His eyes darkened. Score one for me, she thought. Michael also couldn't stand the thought that he might not completely control every woman he wanted to.

"You're being a little idiotic, Katherine."

She put ice into her words then.

"Am I? Sorry, I'll stop. And instead of calling you a fool, I'll settle for calling your little Miss McCullough a scheming, dangerous little snake and tell you where I caught her last night. Are you ready? In the disposal room soothing Peggy and promising she'd soon have her out of there. That was after she'd conned our friend Luczynski into taking her on a tour of Ward One, including a visit to the EC you operated on this morning."

It had the effect she wanted. His anger evaporated, replaced instantly by anxiety he couldn't hide.

She didn't give him a chance to speak. "Michael, I do hope you're just getting well laid and aren't in love with Susan, because we'd be much better off if we put her where we could control her and at the same time still get work out of her. If you understand me. And I think you do."

He flushed and his tone was harsh. "You're out of your mind."

"No, Michael, just practical."

"I'm running this program, not you."

"Wrong again. You *were* running it. That was when you were needed. Now you're not needed any longer, or haven't you noticed? Flemming's theories are going to produce greater results far faster than yours, and Toni Soong is quite competent to do the surgery if you won't."

He'd turned white. "Toni wouldn't touch Susan."

"Oh, I agree she has scruples. She also has a secret case on me, and I suspect I only have to say yes for her to toss her scruples out the window. It might even be a pleasure—she's very attractive."

She ignored his murderous look, waited while the waiter poured more wine, and then said, "I don't like ultimatums, Michael, and I'm sorry to give one to you of all people, believe me, but you will do a severance on Susan McCullough before the week is over."

"Or else . . . ?" The words were barely audible.

"Or else I'll have to have a frank talk with Burnleigh."

"What the hell do you expect him to do?"

"Do? Silly question, Michael. You know as well as I how paranoid he is about security. One word to him and I suspect it will be good-bye Susan, courtesy of some old friend from his CIA days. And good-bye at the same time to Flemming's AAD theory, and with it all your dreams and hopes. Flemming wouldn't work without her. He's already made that quite clear, hasn't he?"

Michael managed a harsh laugh. "Forget it, Katherine. Burnleigh may think the world of you, but I'm still his man and always will be."

"Of course, Michael. I'm not his man, how could I be? But as a woman I do have a certain leverage you don't have and which you might as well know right now I haven't hesitated to use for the last several years"—she smiled slightly—"in spite of some of his rather strange predilections."

He stared, disbelieving. "You bitch."

She shrugged. "Sorry, Michael. It's what's known as taking care of number one, and I wouldn't be so sure if I were you that Burnleigh would want to give up what I do for him in order to please you—or anybody else, for that matter."

She watched his confidence evaporate. And inwardly exulted. She'd won, she knew. He'd swallowed her lie about sleeping with Burnleigh and had nothing to trump her with. She wondered why she'd ever had an anxious moment.

He suddenly looked gray and haggard. She put her hand over his again. "Look, Michael, we're old friends. Let's not talk about it any more this evening. Let's have dessert and some fun. We could go to that late-night jazz club we used to get so charged up on, remember? All those dark lights and sexy blues music. I'm out with the most attractive man in town and I don't want the evening ever to be over."

She refrained from asking whose apartment he would prefer to make love in. His or hers. That would come later.

Instead, she just caressed his motionless hand and smiled.

31

John was desperately tired. He could not ever remember anything like it. It was as though half his mind simply refused to function. He kept wanting only to sleep. Forever. How wonderful it would be to do so, simply to will himself to die and then do it.

Except he couldn't die, or sleep. He had to keep going at any cost. Thank God for phenmetrazine, although he could tell Susan was cheating him. He reckoned the last two days she'd cut him down to twenty-five milligrams, but he'd got around that by complaining violently to Katherine that he couldn't work with so much Thorazine in him. Miraculously, she'd reduced his dosage and thus maintained the balance.

Sleep and surrender still came at him in waves, however. He fought back desperately, using all the new and heightened abilities of his own brain, all the new physiological awareness of his own cortex, the endless new neuron circuitry that had been dormant in his old life and was now so hyperactive.

And he was very close to finding what he'd looked so long and so hard for. There seemed to be only one hurdle left, some sort of snag he couldn't understand. Just before he'd started taking the phenmetrazine, he'd achieved a major breakthrough in identifying the password's elusive "extent." That meant he had found at least the country where the phone was located. Now, in three completely sleepless nights and days, he'd discovered the "block," or area code, of the number and then the "files" and "records" in which were stored the district of the number and the number itself.

All he needed was to feed the mainframe with the correct designation for each and it would surrender the number's ten-letter alpha version. The password he sought would finally be his.

He had done just that. Triumphant.

And waited.

A flash of green print. "Invalid."

Impossible. He queried Mainframe again. Same answer.

And again. "Invalid."

He couldn't believe it. Someplace he'd failed. Where, in the name of God? Check it out.

And he had. All morning. And all afternoon, too, while Susan covered for him with EEG work. Time and again while he hid his rising panic from her, he'd gone through all his work a dozen times, looking for some tiny mistake. He found none. It was perfect. Time and again the mainframe agreed and told him he was okay.

And then, each time he'd type in the verified alpha designations, run it in the verified sequence, the same electronic word would magically appear with awful defeating finality against the deep gray of his terminal's cathode-ray tube.

"Invalid."

Now Susan was gone and the tube stared silently back at him, opaque, the green letters unblinking. The hum of his console's electric motor vibrated faintly through the exhausted cells of his brain like an echo of doom.

How the hell had they rigged it? Did it need some special key to make it work? A special additional code to unlock the coded password? And if so, what sort of code? How complex?

Behind him, the lights of his life-sustaining monitor winked steadily in green and red. Through the open door of the homeroom he could see Rachel, Helen, and Annette. They had started their rest period.

He'd persuaded the nurse to allow him more working time, but there'd be no rest for him when it was over if he hadn't succeeded. He had to keep going now, no matter what. Because soon they'd come and get him, the doctors. He could tell, he hadn't long left. One evening like this, tomorrow or the next day, they'd take him away from his supposed neurometrics. But not to the homeroom. They'd take him to the disposal room instead, and put Susan in his place. One more head on a pole. The new-girl soccer ball. With orders to win. Think, Susan McCullough, think as you've never thought before, or we'll pull the plug on you. And put your extracted brain halves on the cold polished zinc of an anatomy table to be sliced into thin sections so we can see what made you tick.

Then, all of a sudden, with no warning as to why, he saw it. Clearly. Blindingly. The key.

So very, very simple.

Simple because the mind that had created it was simple. Not complex and devious like his own, but very ordinary. A mind without a personality, a mind which couldn't have fun and say things like "Try again, stupid," or "Go screw," but had to resort instead to mundane pronouncements like "Invalid" or "Password?"

Encoding should be complicated, hard to decrypt. So what does a boring simple mind think is complicated? Backwards is complicated. Encode it one way, decode it in reverse.

Lock it up with area, district, and number designations all in proper order.

Unlock it in reverse order, the letters for the number becoming the letters for the area and the district.

John's mind raced. He programmed in his head, typed the program into his terminal, ran it.

He waited.

One second, two.

Green print again dashed across the dark gray cathode-ray tube, luminescent.

"TRIBYSADUN."

He stared, almost not believing it. It worked. The password was revealed.

Triumph. He'd done it. He'd won. TRIBYSADUN. All he had to do was type it out and order Mainframe to transmit to TELENET the lengthy and damning memorandum numbered 19479B waiting in its Goliath memory. And do it right away. Now. Tomorrow could be too late. Don't wait another second.

He flicked his tongue switch, activating a broadcast to the homeroom. There was audio watch there and he'd be heard, but the nurse probably wouldn't understand, and even if he did, who cared? It would be too late. Rachel and Helen and Annette had to know.

"Rachel! Helen! Success. I've got it. Just this moment. It's going out now."

He put his lips back to his sip-puff tube, sucking the familiar hardness of it. "Transmit 19479B to TELENET. TRIBYSADUN."

He waited. One second, two. Green letters flowed on the terminal's gray screen below his own message.

"Password invalid."

He stared, disbelieving, then, barely thinking, typed out his order again. He might have made a typing error.

But again: "Password invalid."

His triumph shattered. What was wrong? He had to succeed. Dammit, he had to. Okay, don't panic. He was nearly there at least. He'd find the problem. It was probably quite simple.

He typed carefully. "Verify search procedure."

And typed in the backwards designated numbers again.

"Search procedure correct."

"Verify password location."

"Location correct."

"TRIBYSADUN is password."

"Invalid."

What the hell! Had Mainframe gone crazy? It didn't make sense.

Or did it?

Suddenly, something in TRIBYSADUN leapt at him. Scrambled letters that meant something else quite clear. Unscrambled—you got BRAIN STUDY. What could fit Borg-Harrison's program better?

Almost simultaneously, something further clicked in his memory. A word from far back. TRIBYSADUN was a drug, wasn't it? Five or six years ago? Yes, of course. An experimental tricyclic antidepressant put out by the English drug company of Saford and Dunfrey. There'd been trouble, some hospital deaths, they'd pulled it off the market.

So he was dealing with an anagram. A relatively simple twist he should have been prepared for.

He heard Helen's voice. Urgent. "John? Have you done it? What's happening?"

And Annette and Rachel. "John? John?"

"Almost," he answered. "Right place, right word, too, but with a twist to it. May have to use its anagram instead."

He gripped his sip-puff tube between his lips again, ready to type another message.

A sudden sharp pain stabbed high into the left

side of his head. What was that? He waited—half-surprised, half-frightened. The pain ebbed.

It was nothing. Nothing at all. A twinge. Forget it. He began his message. "Verify TRIBYSADUN is—"

And the pain hit again, intensified like a knife thrust. Stayed.

His tongs? Had one pierced his skull? A redness dotted the cathode-ray tube. The tube or his eyes? He could hardly see his terminal screen. What had he just typed? He couldn't remember. He'd have to begin again.

"Scratch message."

"Okay."

He lipped the sip-puff tube. And got no further. The misty red screen became darker and darker.

Rushing into blackness now. With the pain agonizing. And there was wind. Roaring wind. And falling.

Then silence.

32

Susan came into the neurometric lab exactly ten minutes later. Cleaning up her desk downstairs, she had come across a formula John had frequently asked for. It was a ready excuse for coming back. What she really wanted was to plead with him once more to take a break and sleep, even if just for one rest period. He was looking so awful.

In the twilight of the computer-crammed little room she saw that John's eyes were closed and knew immediately that he was gone. There was a look of peace on his face. Peace and death. And this time death would be forever.

There was a gravestone in the cemetery with his name on it. She had gone nearly every Sunday to leave flowers there, and she would soon go there again. She touched his cheek with her fingers. She lifted her hood and brushed her lips against his forehead, still life-warm from his console, but his flesh unresponsive.

She tried to think how she felt, couldn't. A kind of numbness, a kind of pain at the same time. But not like his first death. Not the darkness of total despair. She felt only a deep, almost overwhelming sadness. And at the same time a strange relief. Hell for John was finally over. Wherever he was, wherever he'd gone, could not be worse than where he'd been.

Then she heard Helen's voice, electronic and urgent. How many times had Helen called her? "Susan, Susan!"

And Rachel. "Susan. Quickly."

She went to the homeroom. Helen's eyes were desperate. "Susan, hurry, before they know he's died and come for him."

"Maybe for you this time," Rachel hissed.

"John said he found the password," Helen said.

"Just before he went." That was Annette. "He said there was a twist to it. Something about an anagram."

Words spilled uncontrolled from all three now, desperate and ignoring the audio watch.

"Find it, Susan. It's on his terminal. Hurry."

And then from Rachel, "Too late. He's heard."

Her console was facing the observation window. Following her look, Susan saw the nurse on his feet heading for the neurometric lab, a sense of urgency about him. The germ-lock doors thudded, there was his muffled exclamation. He appeared beside her.

"When did it happen?"

He didn't wait for an answer. He went back to the

observation room and his desk and grabbed his telephone.

"Hurry, Susan. Don't just stand there."

"Before they come and stop you."

She left them and went back to John and the tiny lab. It was suddenly all a dream. Unreal. The head on the console wasn't John. It was just some wax dummy. John was tall and slender and draped his feet and legs on desks and almost never combed his thick rumpled hair. And he made biting, cynical remarks and loved her and Percival and the human race.

She flicked his power switch to "Off."

The room was at once eerily silent. How long would it be before the nurse realized something was seriously wrong?

Almost hesitantly she went to the terminal, pressed "Recall" and asked for John's last input.

Green letters appeared as though by magic. "Verify TRIBYSADUN . . ."

She stared. The ECs were right. There it was. And all John's killing work to find it. But what a peculiar word, if it was a word! It didn't make sense. She ought to check it first of all. She typed in, "Please comply with verification request."

The terminal answered immediately. "TRIBYSA-DUN is correct."

As it did, she almost simultaneously saw the anagram Annette said John had discovered. TRIBY-SADUN was simply BRAIN STUDY. She had the mainframe memory file number for John's memorandum. All she had to do was recall it, add the password, and order Mainframe to transmit.

She felt a nearly irrepressible excitement and relief. But wait—which would be the password? The anagram or BRAIN STUDY itself? Or was BRAIN STUDY the anagram?

Either one—do it.

She typed in, "Transmit 19479B to TELENET, TRIBYSADUN."

She sat back. Green letters flowed again.

Invalid.

Okay, then it was BRAIN STUDY. She typed in a new order, waited.

Invalid.

"Invalid?" She felt stirrings of panic. She fought them back. Keep calm. Investigate. And face the truth, come directly to the point. She typed in, "Is TRIBYSADUN password?"

"No."

She hesitated, took a deep breath and typed, "Is BRAIN STUDY password?"

The answer had to be yes. But it wasn't. There were instant green letters that said "No."

She stared in complete disbelief. That couldn't be possible. John had uncovered TRIBYSADUN. He said he'd found the password. John was never wrong. Never. And what about the anagram? BRAIN STUDY couldn't be just a coincidence. It was too real, too natural.

The panic exploded, seized her whole body, froze her mind. She glanced through the open door of the homeroom at the ECs, waiting in silent expectation.

Then at John, so waxen and unreal on his console, his vital-signs monitor inactive, its life-telling lines all flat or nonexistent.

Control your emotions, McCullough. Think clearly. Use your brains. That's what John would have said.

Very carefully she typed, "What is TRIBYSA-DUN?"

"Sorry. Classified."

It was too much. Frustration screamed through her. She hit the terminal with her clenched fist. Goddamned machine. Damn you to hell. What's going on?

She didn't get further. The germ-lock door thudded and the nurse reappeared, this time with Toni Soong, who went at once to John.

"Oh, my God, no." She turned wide eyes on Susan. "I'm so sorry."

All Susan's resolve crumbled. The terminal and the code were forgotten. John became everything again. She gestured helplessly.

Toni came and put an arm around her. "You poor thing. You should have called me at once, not stayed here alone with him." She gently steered Susan away. "Don't look anymore, Susan. Let us take care of him now, okay?" She turned back to John, taking her medical flashlight from her white coat and beginning an immediate examination.

Susan found herself in the homeroom with the ECs and heard Helen speaking low and urgently. "Did you do it?"

She shook her head numbly. She didn't care. John was dead, they had killed him. Just as surely as if they'd pulled the switch, the way Michael had with Judge Thurston. Medical experiments on machines. Used-up things to be disposed of when no longer useful. She felt a sudden and almost inexpressible rage.

Then Michael himself appeared. And Katherine. The nurse must have alerted them, too. The little lab had so many people in it she couldn't see John anymore. Maybe they'd already taken him away.

Michael came in and said, "Are you all right, Susan?"

She was calm. "No, I'm not. And don't pretend you care. How did he die?"

He gave her a quick look. "We're not sure yet, but probably a subarachnoid hemorrhage resulting from an aneurism."

They'd take him to the autopsy room, she thought, and find out. They'd split his skull, remove his brain, and slice it open for microscopic examination. She felt terror rise in her throat. Not John. Anybody else. But not John.

"I don't want him cut up."

"Take it easy, Susan."

"You're not going to cut him up, goddammit!" It was a scream. "Not John."

Suddenly Katherine was there. "Susan, get hold of yourself."

She flung Katherine off. "Lying bitch. Murderer!" Her backhand blow caught Katherine across her mouth, and then she went for her, tearing at her face, screaming.

"Susan!" Michael dragged her back, pinned both her arms. There were bubbling weals on Katherine's face, and blood trickled from her split mouth. Susan tried to shake loose, couldn't. Michael's grip was iron. "You too, you bastard. Let go of me!" She flailed at his shins with her heels.

He said sharply to Toni Soong. "Toni, quick!" And dragged Susan out through the germ lock.

In the control room, she kept struggling, hearing her own voice over and over. "Murderers!"

Then Toni suddenly reappeared, moving quickly, all smooth professionalism, and she felt the needle jab into her arm. Expertly. She stopped kicking and fighting and stared incredulous down at the hypodermic, the plunger sliding fast down the tube and the drug disappearing.

It worked at once. Almost while she was still looking at it. She managed to say, "You rotten bastards, all of you." The words felt instantly thick to her, as though her tongue were swollen. And Toni became distant, as though a room length away instead of right there.

Michael, too. She heard him say, "Get a stretcher." She tried to speak again, couldn't. Words in her mind wouldn't translate to her lips and tongue. They had put her in a chair, and she tried to rise, but her limbs were leaden and now she saw Michael, too, like Toni, at the end of a long tunnel.

I'm going to faint, she thought.

She didn't feel frightened. She only felt helpless. She could hardly see anymore. What they said was a meaningless jumble. She was floating on a calm sea of warm water. Not her body, just her head.

She seemed to float forever, and heads bobbed in

the sea around her. Who were they? And how could they be there? If you were just a head, you were held by surgical tongs over a machine and made to think. Or else.

"Sleep," one of them said softly. "Sleep."

Susan closed her eyes and let the darkness flow in around her.

33

Walter Burnleigh had never liked informers. He made no exception for the one who was now in his office, even though what the man had just told him was alarming. He turned away from Al Luczynski, seated nervously across his desk, to look out the window at the trees lining Massachusetts Avenue, visible across the lawn and driveway of the Borg-Harrison headquarters.

Late summer was on them, and he knew it had to be hot outside, but knowing it failed to remove the chill of anxiety he felt. What he'd just heard was in fact not only a threat to the whole brain-research program; his own position and reputation could also be in serious jeopardy.

Luczynski had told a story which seemed to indicate more than Katherine's ambitions getting the better of her, something he'd sensed for some time was happening. It seemed to indicate she'd lost all reasonable judgment as well. When he'd given her

unofficial tacit permission to procure ECs in an unorthodox manner, he'd never expected she would go
beyond terminals who hadn't volunteered or borderline cases who stood a slight chance to survive. Susan
McCullough was neither. She wasn't even ill. She was
a healthy, vibrant young woman, and putting her on
a console would be tantamount to murder. And what
about Michael? He must have gone mad to have
reached the point of doing such a thing, especially to
a woman with whom he'd been having an affair.

Burnleigh brought his attention back to Al Luczynski and swung his chair around to face him again.
Tension at the lab had to be at flash point for him to
have elected to play informer. His doing so now
posed an additional threat to the program. Who
knew to whom he'd talk next? They'd lost his loyalty,
clearly, and he'd have to be put under round-the-
clock surveillance the same as McCullough.

As Burnleigh looked at his big bearded face, his
chill of anxiety intensified. Luczynski hadn't come
to rescue Susan McCullough. He'd expressed no
outrage at what Katherine planned, not even an objec-
tion. He seemed completely untroubled by the pros-
pect of Susan having her head removed, and obviously was there only to protect his own skin. Could one
become so inured to medical horror as to become
immune to it? What about himself? What point had
he himself reached? When they started the program,
he'd hardly been able to bring himself even to look
at photographs of their first few severances. Only
the possibility of success, and with it a revolution
in human development, justified the use their pro-

DAVID OSBORN

gram made of human life. Now he found himself thinking of the ECs merely as non-human experiments. It was a shock to realize he'd perhaps become as immune to horror as Luczynski.

He said perfunctorily, "When is the operation scheduled for, Doctor?"

"Tomorrow morning. Seven-thirty."

"I see. Now to you. You mentioned other nonvolunteers—Dr. Flemming, a nurse—and a trend toward similar recruits through the hospital-records computer network. Why haven't you resigned?"

"Well . . ." Luczynski hesitated.

Burnleigh offered him a warm smile he didn't feel. "Security, right? You're worried we might not let you go?"

The anesthesiologist seemed relieved it was out in the open. "Yes, sir. That, and where else would I get work now? Without a reference and without revealing what I've been doing for five years."

Burnleigh turned his smile into a relaxed laugh. "Neither presents any problem to me at all, Dr. Luczynski. Borg-Harrison is not a Russian gulag. You've proven your loyalty ten times over by coming here to talk to me, and your medical record is excellent. I would have no trouble in recommending you highly for any job you wanted and in slanting your medical record with us any way you liked. How about a senior position at Bethesda? I still have considerable influence with the Navy. Or if you wanted, an administrative position in Mass General or Columbia Presbyterian?"

He waited. Kicking someone upstairs had always

266

solved similar problems. He was certain it would with the anesthesiologist.

He wasn't disappointed. Luczynski suddenly grinned and literally heaved a sigh of relief. "Thank you, sir. Bethesda would be just fine. I like Washington."

Five minutes later, he left. Burnleigh stared at the heavy oak door he'd closed behind him. So much for the informer. The situation was bad, and basically his own fault. No matter what, he should have kept a much closer eye on Katherine and possibly even risked using the vast resources of the VA.

His eyes fell on the silver-framed photo of his wife that dominated one side of his desk. Regardless of the exigencies of past jobs, the Navy at war, the covert operations of the CIA, necessary political hatchet jobs he'd performed for the White House, he'd always tried to tailor his actions to those he thought would not bring about Eleanor Burnleigh's disapproval. She was a moral woman, a loving wife and doting grandmother, and although over the years life had taught her to bend personal feelings upon occasion, she had always drawn a certain line.

Well, he would also draw a line. And immediately. It was never too late to set things straight. They'd use the VA and get the lab back on course. But first McCullough would have to be rescued, then effectively silenced and kept on the job. He could double her salary for a start. Everyone had a price.

He buzzed his secretary. "Get me Dr. Blair, please." Moments later, Katherine replied.

"I understand we've lost Flemming," he said.

Her hesitation gave her away. He'd caught her by surprise. She was clearly wondering how he knew, and also wondering whether or not to ask him how.

Then she said, "Unfortunately, yes. I was planning to call you about it shortly."

"How close was he to success?"

"Very close."

"Do you think McCullough can finish it up?"

She hesitated again, then said, "Yes, I do."

Obviously, he thought, she was also preparing not to ask his permission about Susan and to cook up some sort of story to cover herself.

Either that or Luczynski had been lying. Burnleigh was certain the anesthesiologist had been telling the truth. Should he reveal what more he knew or not? Doing so would also tip off the presence of an informer, and he wasn't sure that was wise.

"Good," he said. "But she must be upset by Flemming's death. She won't want to quit, will she?"

"I think she can be persuaded not to."

"Is she still involved with Michael?"

"I think so, yes, sir."

"Well, that might help. All right, then, Katherine. I'd like to talk with the young lady, let her know Borg-Harrison is behind her with everything we've got. That sort of thing. Give her morale a boost. How about bringing her up here next Monday?"

There was dead silence. He wanted to laugh out loud. Don't try playing chess with me, Katherine Blair. I win.

Then she said. "Fine. What's a good time?"

He glanced at his calendar. "I think we'll take her

out to lunch. Come by here about twelve-thirty. Both of you. I'll ask my secretary to reserve a table at the Caucus Room. They serve an excellent soufflé."

"Very well, sir. I'll see you Monday."

"And Katherine?"

"Yes, sir?"

"Don't forget to give Miss McCullough my condolences."

"Yes, sir."

Burnleigh put down the receiver, made a note on his calendar, and allowed himself a moment's self-congratulation. Katherine would suspect he was onto her and take his stand on McCullough as a warning. With luck, he would have to do nothing else. If Michael needed controlling, she would do it herself. Everyone had his weakness, and Katherine's was her ambition. In one short stroke he'd almost certainly rescued the brain-research program from disaster.

It was one of the few times in his career that he was wrong.

Katherine put down the receiver of the phone in her office and seethed. There was no way of pulling Susan out of the drugged condition she was in and excusing it later by saying they'd tranquilized her for her own good. Even if they could talk her out of her reaction to Judge Thurston, and the disposal room, and her grief over Flemming, how could they explain her shaven head and the indelible cutting line already painted across her lower throat?

Katherine cursed. Who had told him about Flemming? Al? Toni? Sara? Some other nurse? Had they told him about Susan, also? She suspected they had. It didn't matter, the damage was done. They would have to go ahead with the severance regardless of Burnleigh.

But it was doubly infuriating because she'd planned so carefully. She had skillfully redirected Michael's guilt at what she was forcing him to do into hostility against Susan herself. He was showing no visible qualms about the operation.

Where Burnleigh was concerned, she'd planned to disclaim any responsibility if he reacted adversely. Michael was still titular head of the lab and she'd been prepared to insist she was only taking orders from him. She was confident that in a toss-up between herself and Michael, she would win. She'd never met a man who couldn't be seduced, and she'd been quite prepared to turn her claims to Michael of an affair with Burnleigh into a reality.

Now all that was out of the question. Burnleigh would be too livid at being defied to be influenced. She could no longer say the severance was Michael's doing, for there would be no excuse for not warning Burnleigh that Michael was defiantly going ahead with it. Adding it up, she realized she would have to adopt a backup plan which would use up a trump card she had been saving for some future date.

Every man had his Achilles' heel, Burnleigh no less than others. Once, over lunch, he had inadvertently revealed the identity of his chief adversary on the Borg-Harrison board of directors. The man was the president of the powerful Union Credit and Commercial Trust Company and apparently, more than anything, wanted Burnleigh's position for the political influence it would give him.

If Burnleigh got rough with her, she could get equally rough back. And she was fully prepared to. Her reward for filling in the bank president on every detail of what was going on would almost certainly be equal to if not better than anything Burnleigh had offered her. In the same stroke she would absolve herself of any guilt with the man who would then almost certainly take Burnleigh's place.

As for whoever had blown the whistle—and the more she thought of it, the more she was sure it was Al Luczynski—he would never believe she'd dare defy Admiral Burnleigh. When the severance went ahead as planned, Luczynski would take it for granted it was with Burnleigh's sanction and stay quiet to reap whatever reward Burnleigh had promised him for his silence.

Katherine glanced at her watch. There were only about fourteen hours left before Susan was where she wanted her. They'd accelerate her recovery; they'd probably need her for only a few months and could easily risk early burnout. Unless something totally unexpected happened—and Katherine could foresee no such thing—the program would be back in high gear tomorrow. And whatever the consequences, she would be on top.

Feeling much better, Katherine headed for Ward One.

34

Only impressions.

Yet another head floated by. Al Luczynski's. Face unsmiling, and above his beard, his eyes dark and unreadable.

Why was he there? He was an anesthesiologist. And was he still angry with her for using him?

There were murmured voices. His and a woman's. A nurse? The sea receded. There was a room around her, the rustle of starched white, a strange blond face. And firm fingers wrapping cloth tightly around her arm. Blood pressure.

"She's looking okay." That was Luczynski again. He must be there to put her to sleep. Had she been in an accident?

Cool air on her body, a hand against her hip. Something stung. A shot?

"See you in the morning, Susan." Brusque, impersonal, he must hate her.

Another head, Katherine Blair. "Hello, Susan."

Hair tied back. A cold smile. Her mouth had been bloody, a thin line of hate. When was that?

Her own voice, her tongue like cotton. "Where's Michael?"

Michael had told her to sign something. He'd put a pen in her hand. She wanted to know what. She had the right. She struggled to see again. A blur focused. Shining wavelets became muted lights. A hospital bed, curtains half-drawn around it. A strange sound. A low humming noise. Something electric.

Drifting away, then. Trying not to, but surrendering.

And floating once more on a calm warm sea with a pale sun above. Just her head bobbing. Helen, too. Hello, Helen. What did you say? John found the password? I know, but it wasn't, and I couldn't figure out why not.

The sea is salt and full of tears, John is dead, and I can't save you. Sorry.

"Lift up, there's a good girl."

Hands touching her head. Small round pressures. Electrodes? Why? There's nothing wrong with my head. I've just had some sort of accident.

Had she fallen? A skull fracture?

John had had an accident. And lost his body and gone to hell.

Helpless. If you were a head, you were helpless too. But she wasn't terminal. Or a volunteer. So it was all right. Heads were other people, executed by a scalpel. Silent, razor-sharp, first through skin like magic, then flesh, then muscle. Gushing blood vessels. Clamps, please. Electric saws for reluctant vertebrae. And crushing rongeurs. Next, operating microscope down for nerves. Thin white delicate hairs.

A body bag and a plastic box, finally. For the undertaker.

But not for her. All that was for the girl she'd seen years ago. Head shaved, throat painted, ready for decapitation.

Poor John. Why couldn't she make his password work? All those hours and hours he'd spent for nothing.

She struggled again to move. The room swam around her, steadied. She was alone. There were green lines and tiny lights.

She forced her eyes to focus. Reflections. That's what. On the glass window of the door. But from where? Concentrate. And on the noise, faint but very close.

She saw a multichannel monitor on a wheeled table right by her head. Its back was to her. That's where the noise came from. And the lights. They were EEG, pulse, temperature, blood pressure, and EKG. Constant readings. Vital signs. Hers.

She got one leg over the edge of the bed. She sat up. And swayed. She was so drugged. Something tugged at her head. She put her hand up. Electrodes. Wires. Her scalp was smooth.

She fell back. The sea returned with its bobbing heads. Calm, flat, quiet. A burnished mirror for a pale sun. She had to try once more to open the trapdoor. Had to figure out how.

A rumbling sound, then. Waves? Thunder? The

calm sea disappeared. The room came back. The sound again. A heavy bumping.

She turned her head. Something big slowly passed the open door, a nurse pushing.

Another nurse said, "What's up?"

"Dr. Soong wants it in Op by seven."

And violence exploded in her. Instantly. A terrible unnamed current. One second it was all a strange blurred dream. The next there was crystal clarity. The room and its objects in sharp focus. Her thoughts with the razor edge of total shock.

She saw what they were pushing—a console. It was for her. They were going to cut off her body, bury tongs in her skull, and hang her above it.

The two nurses disappeared down the corridor and she remembered it all. She'd been there before. The young woman, head shaved, a red incision line across her neck, lying in the same bed in the same room.

Get out. Now! It's your life.

Her heart raced. She heaved up, legs dangling off the bed again. She stood. The room swam. She forced concentration, looked around.

How?

There was her bed, the oxygen unit on the wall by the head of it. Beyond were the monitor and the nurse's table with its tray of drugs and medicine.

What could help her? Suddenly she knew. The monitor. If she could only hang on.

Move quickly. Find the strength before someone came. First, any single-pronged jack plugged into the back of the monitor. The ones for her respiratory reading were closest. There were two. Pull one out, carefully.

Next, the power plug. Pull it out just far enough so that it still fed the monitor with power while letting her slip the point of the jack between its two electricity-charged prongs. But not yet.

Now, the jar of alcohol. On the nurse's desk. The one they kept thermometers in.

She reached, but her strength began to fly away. The room swam around her again. She sank back on the bed.

Stay awake. Don't go back to the sea and float. Stay awake. It's your life. She waited. The sea was warm and calm. Heads bobbing once more. "Hello, Helen. Why doesn't John's password work?"

A sound. The sea disappeared. A nurse adjusting her sheets. Then at the nurse's table. The scrape of a chair as she sat down.

Too late. She'd lost her chance.

But suddenly an urgent sound. A sharp intake of breath. The telephone rattled. Panic in the nurse's voice. "Doctor? I'm getting a very erratic respiratory reading." Silence. Then, "Yes, ma'am. Nalline. Right away. To counteract her Demerol. Yes, Doctor."

The phone slammed down. The nurse was back. Leaning over the bed at the oxygen unit. Susan felt the oxygen cone and pure cool life over her face.

She opened her eyes. A flash of white uniform. The nurse back at her table. Rattling sounds. A drug vial being opened. She had to fight back. But it was too late. The nurse was by her bed again, piggyback-ing the vial into her IV line.

Two seconds, three. And then something jolted. Inside. Like a giant hand. A kind of instant tremendous surging. And her mind was clear again and understanding just what had happened. When she'd pulled the respiratory jack on the monitor, her reading had gone crazy. They thought she was suffering acute respiratory failure and the shot was to bring her out of it.

A flash of white coat. Dark hair, a small figure. Toni Soong came in on the run. She threw one fast glance at the monitor and was at the bed, stethoscope out.

Its cold ear touched Susan's chest. Toni listened, intent, eyes surprised. "Susan?"

One of her eyelids was lifted. A bright light blinded.

"Susan. Do you hear me?"

Don't answer. Let her find out.

"What the Christ is going on?"

Toni and the nurse at the monitor. Toni grabbed her chart off the nurse's table. "Pulse sixty-eight. Temperature 97.1, B.P. 125/80. Pupils reactive." She slammed the chart down. "It's the fucking monitor, and for Christ's sake, we've given her enough Nalline to keep her awake for a year. Fix me 100 Demerol. And call Dr. Luczynski. Tell him it's urgent. He's in the cafeteria."

Move now. Last chance.

It was easy. She rolled over, jammed the respiratory jack between the prongs of the partially released power plug. A loud pop. A blue flame hissed, sparked.

Toni saw. "Jesus!" She started fast around the monitor. "Susan!"

Legs over the bed edge. Shove. The monitor's wheeled table rolled hard into Toni.

Susan stood. Her IV lines yanked loose from her arms, the poles crashing. Electrodes ripped from her scalp.

The rest happened fast. The nurse's shocked look, Toni trying to get around the monitor. Susan grabbed the nurse's thermometer jar, dashed its alcohol on the shorting wires.

A bright flash of light. The nurse's scream. Toni jumping back. One second, two. She tore the oxygen cone from her face, shoved it onto the fire.

A blinding whoosh. Bright orange to the ceiling. Her own hand dancing with flames that pierced pain. She shoved it into the bedcovers, leapt backward, crashing into a chair, fell, got up. Her legs were suddenly like springs, her arms steel. The nurse came for her, raging.

"Leave her!" That was Toni. "Get an extinguisher."

And Toni tearing covers from the bed, trying to smother the flames. The bed curtains flaring up.

In the corridor outside, Susan watched the nurse race for the fire station. She only had minutes—they'd have the fire out in no time. And there was only one place to go. The operating theater was directly opposite. She ducked into it.

Silence. Subdued lights. No one. Shining equipment. Waiting. A sense of urgent expectancy. It was in the operating table and in the anesthesiologist's cart with its gas bottles and tubes and dials. It came

278

from the surgical trolleys with their scores of sterilized instruments wrapped in cloth: bipolar cauteries, retractors, lancets, scalpels, forceps, hemostats. She felt it in the operating microscope and the Carm fluoroscope with its TV screen above the table where she would rest while Michael Burgess cut.

It was there in the life-sustaining console she'd be placed on.

And in a corner in the long narrow blue plastic box that awaited her headless dead body.

She took it all in for less than five seconds; then legs, miraculously still alive, ran to the surgical locker room.

She closed the door behind her and stopped dead, face to face with Katherine.

It couldn't be. But it was. She had removed her clothes and laid them on a bench and was standing in just her underpants and bra by a locker. Her titian hair fell about her shoulders and she looked slender and young and very beautiful.

Her eyes were wide at seeing Susan.

It all happened then like lightning. Susan thought: You're getting ready to watch Michael cut off my head. And without thinking, she moved. Fast. A vague flashed memory. Football in the cold prairie schoolyard. Boys' shouts and cries. Herself, trying to belong. Hit the runner low and hard. Her shoulder slammed into Katherine's stomach, there was the sick crack of the woman's head on the hard tile wall right behind her. They both went down, Katherine over the bench.

Susan rose. Katherine didn't move. There was blood on the back of her head.

A voice somewhere, distantly. The operating room? A door opened and shut. Silence again.

She knew what to do then. She quickly put on Katherine's surgical clothes, hanging in the locker. And a surgical cap and mask. There was a hood, too, with a face plate. She took it and went out into the ward lobby.

The duty nurse looked up. "I've got a fire signal from pre-op, Doctor. What's happened?"

Say something. Answer. She thinks you're Katherine. Her tongue felt like cotton. "It was just a VS monitor short circuit. It's out already." Don't say more. Your voice will give you away.

She waved, went as casually as she could into the main hall, trying to make her walk look natural.

The elevator security guard wasn't there. Probably he'd gone to help with the fire. She crossed the hall and went down the corridor to the Ward Two control room. Just as she reached the door, she heard the elevator arriving. She turned her head slightly to look. Al Luczynski came out and went toward Ward One, pausing an instant as he saw her.

Time stopped.

He had to think she was a nurse, or possibly Katherine. He just had to.

And then she became aware of a weight under her arm. The face-plated hood. She'd forgotten to put it on.

Don't rush, don't look frantic. You'll give yourself

away. There's the doorknob. Slip on the hood and go in. Casually.

It was as though someone else moved, not herself. The knob turned, the door gave. She put the hood on as she moved.

Seconds later, the door thudded shut behind her.

The male nurse at the control panel half-turned. "Good morning, Doctor."

She didn't answer. Couldn't. She didn't have the strength. She stepped toward the germ lock, her legs suddenly water. Don't sway, not now. Not at the last moment.

She forced her body into the germ lock, waiting an instant between its two soundproof doors and in its eerie fluorescent violet light, certain he'd follow her. She might not be so trapped here as if she were in the lab. She had the wild idea she could mutter some excuse and duck around him back into the control room, perhaps lock the door behind her. Then give up John's code search and take a chance there was some way out of the building.

But he didn't come. No glare of light from the control room shattered the violet half-dark of the lock.

She went into the neurometric lab.

35

Al Luczynski had been at his desk for half an hour and, glancing at his watch, realized it was time to go upstairs. They'd be bringing the patient into the operating room any minute now. Katherine had come by his office a few minutes ago—he remembered her saying good morning from the corridor outside his door. She was probably already upstairs and would have something sharp to say if he wasn't on time. He felt a surge of resentment. What the hell was she going to attend the operation for anyway, except to get her own back at Susan? The only other time in a couple of years he could remember her doing that was when they'd done Flemming. Katherine was a shrink. She didn't belong in an operating room for any reason. It was years since she'd done her internship and she didn't know the first thing about techniques developed since then, nor probably remember anything she'd ever learned. Surgery was something you could forget fast. Katherine's presence during Flemming's severance had made both Michael and Toni nervous. They'd probably be even more nervous today.

A few minutes ago, a scrub nurse had come down with a VS printout on Susan. He glanced at it a last time. Heart, temperature, blood pressure, encephalogram readings, respiratory—it was all there and no problem. She wasn't the kind of basket case they usually got; she was healthy as hell. He stuffed the printout in his pocket and went out the door.

In the corridor, he heard his phone ring. That would be Katherine, no doubt. Are you coming, Al? Bitch.

He called the elevator, slotted the doors open with his ID card, and went upstairs.

In the hall when the doors opened again and he got out, he saw a nurse just outside Ward Two. She was in operating gear, cap, gown, and mask. It seemed strange. And instead of wearing her hood, she was carrying it.

Luczynski continued into Ward One, meaning to ask the duty nurse, and found that no one was at the nurse's station. That was also strange. What the hell was going on? Perhaps she was the one who'd gone into Ward Two. Maybe one of the heads had wiped out.

But he ran into the duty nurse the moment he entered the operating room. She seemed flushed and excited.

"What's up?"

"Didn't they reach you on the phone? There was a

fire in pre-op. It's out now, but the patient's run off."

Holy smoke, Luczynski thought. Wait until Katherine gets hold of whoever is responsible. They're really in for it. He grinned at the nurse. "She won't go far. Where's Dr. Soong?"

"A nurse got burned. She's treating her."

"Dr. Blair?"

"She went to alert security and see if she could find the patient."

The nurse headed back to her station, and Luczynski went on to the operating locker room.

Katherine was still crumpled on the floor between the bench and the tile wall. She was half-curled up like a child, her arms crossed over her breasts, her beautiful titian hair falling over her face and hiding her features. For an instant, until he saw her hair, Luczynski didn't register who it was. Then he did.

He stood silently staring at her. And at the empty locker near her and at a hospital gown thrown across the bench. The gown had to be Susan's. And Katherine had to be lying there because of her. His eye fell on the open locker. She must have taken operating-room gear, a cap and gown, maybe even a mask. Thought she could get away disguised. Well, she couldn't, the rotten little bitch. She'd used him, when he'd cared about her. He'd written her a warning message, given her drugs when she'd asked for them, even shown her around the operating area. And all he'd gotten in return was trouble. He'd find her in a minute. Where could she go with a shaved head and drugged half out of her mind? Then Mi-

chael and Toni would damn soon have her smart-
ass head off and on a console and her flopping body
that was too good for anybody in a blue plastic box
headed for the undertaker.

He'd start by looking for her in Ward Two. The
nurse he'd seen go in dressed in surgical clothes
instead of the usual protective clothing and face-
plated hood—that was probably her. What better
place to hide temporarily until her sedation wore
off? Who would think to look for her among the
heads?

He felt an exhilaration he hadn't felt for a long
time. She probably thought she could get away with
it, too. He couldn't wait to see her expression when
he put his hand on her shoulder. "Hello, Miss
McCullough, your Royal Highness. Remember me,
Jackass Luczynski, the court jester?"

A faint moan stopped him. He turned. Katherine.
Lying back there on the floor. He'd almost forgotten
her. Katherine and all the years of bullying and
laughter at his expense: making him feel a fool for
daring to try to get somewhere with her; what she'd
done to Claire. Katherine was more important. Leave
Michael's little whore to the security boys. She
couldn't leave the building without normal clothes.
He'd never have Katherine helpless like this again.
And nobody would ever know. Ever. Except for the
hair, one slender young female head looked like
another, especially when the face was half-covered
with an anesthesia cone.

And the hair was easy. He went to the operating
room and came back with a surgical cap, a hypo-

dermic, and a bottle of Betadine Solution. He moved quickly, professionally at ease. He tucked Katherine's hair up under the cap so it wouldn't be seen, taped the cap to her head. The cap wouldn't be removed until more than halfway through the operation when Toni drilled holes in the skull to receive the pointed ends of the Gardner-Wells tongs which would hold her head rigid over the console.

Next he injected ten cc's of Pentothal into the median vein in her upper forearm, quickly painted an incision line on her neck, and numbered it correctly.

Finally, he slipped off her bra and pants and scooped her up in his arms as though she were a child. All that remained was to put her on the operating table. But he hesitated, aroused suddenly by the warmth of her flesh, the closeness of her breasts, and the sight of her thick triangle of pubic hair. He could finally do anything he wanted to her and she couldn't say no. In seconds he could make her pay for laughing at him when he'd wanted her. He only had to put her down like a rag doll and use her, and if he couldn't make it, he could always pretend he had.

He started to, feeling his whole body flame, and then stopped. There wasn't time. Someone might come.

He quickly carried her into the operating room, strapped her onto the table, and pulled the surgical sheet up over her body. When eventually they discovered who she was, there was no proof and there never would be any that it was he who had put her there. Anyone could have done so.

He stayed, staring at her a last moment or two. Then he left her and went to see what had happened in pre-op and to tell Toni everything was okay.

36

It seemed to Susan she'd been sitting and staring at the terminal in John's lab for her whole life. Ever since she'd come, she'd felt physically and mentally incapable of even the slightest movement. She'd simply sat in the chair before the terminal and done nothing, even though she knew she had to—her life depended on it.

The room was so strange, she thought, without John. Everything was familiar except his absence. For all its computer equipment and medical monitors, the space felt enormous without the big humming console that had kept John alive.

And without John himself. She realized now how he had always dominated wherever he was, even when an EC and helpless.

She tried to move, couldn't. An inner voice shouted: Time's running out! It didn't make any difference.

The intercom from the control room suddenly clicked on, shattering the silence. It was the nurse.

"Doctor, you forgot the log. Do you want me to bring it in?"

Dully she remembered the doctors and nurses usually checked the log before coming into the ward. It was helpful for them to know everything about each EC since their last visit—not just their chart readings, but what their moods had been, what their activities were.

"Doctor?"

She forced an answer. "No. Not necessary."

She hadn't wanted to speak. She could only hope the hood would muffle her voice enough so he couldn't tell she wasn't Katherine.

"Okay, Doctor." The intercom clicked off.

It was what it took to jar her into reality. She had only minutes to act, perhaps even less. They'd have half the building searched by now, and someone was bound to decide she'd gone into Ward Two.

She flicked on her terminal's power switch.

The dark gray cathode-ray tube lightened behind the opaque screen. She took a deep breath. She mustn't think of the terror she'd just left, or that at any moment someone might burst in and drag her back to it. Or of John, or of the others in the homeroom.

She must think only of the computer. All that existed in the world, herself, the terminal, and the mainframe—and how to make John's code word work. Nothing else. It was what she'd come for and her only chance.

She heard Annette's voice. "What's happening?"

And Helen's. "Are you doing it?"

They weren't using her name because the nurse would pick it up over the open audio watch, but they knew she wasn't Katherine or Toni. Either doctor would have gone directly to them, not to John's terminal. When they'd last seen her, she was being taken away, and they would wonder how she got back but would guess why she had.

"Talk to us!"

There wasn't time to answer. She could see Rachel through the open door, her pale, thin, almost-beautiful face, the surgical tongs glinting halo-light, the hideous blue nylon-rubber collar hiding the tubes that came down from her neck stump to the massive chrome console below. And Rachel's dark eyes, burning.

"Can we help?"

She shut out their voices and once again tried transmitting, using first TRIBYSADUN, then BRAIN STUDY.

When the answer each time was the same, "Invalid," she remembered dully that she'd done it before. Neither was the password.

The first wave of nausea hit her then, and with it a sudden sense of sinking back into the sea. The shot they'd given her was wearing off. When it was gone completely, she'd be helpless.

Try to think, Susan. Don't panic again the way you did before. Think.

TRIBYSADUN had to be very important because it was classified. She remembered that, also. And

BRAIN STUDY, too, because it was anagrammatic. So she was almost there. Perhaps it's both words together. Try that. And methodically. Type them in backwards, forwards, in every combination.

Another wave of sickness. Cold sweat dripped beneath the face-plated hood. She was bathed in it. Her fingers typed out a variety of transmissions, one after another. Each time, the answer came back the same.

Invalid.

Invalid.

Invalid.

She sank back in her chair. There were sounds in her head now, and the room swam. What was wrong? Why couldn't she understand? John had once said the mind that thought up the security envelope around the password was a relatively simple one.

The terminal's screen stared silently back at her.

The screen became the sea.

Faceless heads bobbed once more. Voices murmured and babbled. Rachel, Helen, and Annette. "What's happening? Tell us. Are you all right? Can we help?"

Don't float, Susan. Don't. She forced herself back into the lab, to focus on the terminal. Forced it to stop blurring.

Suppose TRIBYSADUN and BRAIN STUDY weren't designators the way she'd assumed them to be, the way they would have to be if they were the password. Suppose instead they were just indicators. Both pointing to something else. Logically, that something else would have to be related to both of them—other- wise they wouldn't exist at all in the security system.

Or—taking it one step further—it could be some- thing that had to do with their anagrammatic rela- tionship with each other. That was also logical. But where did that take her? It ought to be something simple, but she couldn't think. Just couldn't. The sea kept washing back against her mind, bright and calm and burnished.

Dimly she heard Rachel. "Hurry. You're wanted."

She looked up. Through the observation window she saw the nurse on the phone, gesticulating and looking through the window at her. Then she saw him put the receiver down hard and flip his audio- speak switch.

"Dr. Blair? Telephone, Dr. Blair. Can you hear me?"

She didn't reply, and he headed at once for the germ-lock door. It thudded behind as he came in. "Dr. Blair, I guess my audio's nonfunctional. It's Admiral Burnleigh. Dr. Blair?"

She hardly heard him because she suddenly knew the answer. It was simple, so simple. And so very obvious.

"Doctor?"

She found herself laughing uncontrollably.

And the nurse's face plate was suddenly against hers, eyes darkening with recognition. "You're not Dr. Blair. Who the hell are you?"

Her hood snapped back. Cool air rushed her shaved scalp.

"Holy Christ!" Immediately his hands were pulling her away from the terminal. "Okay, enough of this. Let's go."

"No!" She wrenched free. "Not yet! I've got it, John. I've got it." Her fingers pressed keys. "Transmit to TELENET, file 19479B—"

She was yanked to her feet. Hard.

"I said enough, dammit!"

She started to struggle again, gave up. It was too late. She was too weak. And she had come so close.

But from the other room there was suddenly a low moaning howl, a sound like the sound of an injured cat.

Helen's voice then, frantic. "Nurse, it's Annette. Quick!"

The nurse froze.

The sound rose, eerie and horrifying. It was the same sound Peggy had made. Cursing, the nurse let go of Susan and went to the homeroom.

Susan's legs gave way. She fell back in the chair before the terminal, head bowed.

She barely heard Rachel's hiss. "Hurry. Last chance."

Her arms were lead. And her eyelids. The keys and terminal screen blurred. She got one hand up to the keyboard.

Very slowly, letter by letter, one letter after the other, she typed, "ANAGRAM."

For a last time words flowed in a green line across the screen.

"Received and transmitting."

The trapdoor opened, the message went out to the world.

But the sea came back to Susan and she was unaware. Just as she was unaware that Annette abruptly stopped howling and winked at Rachel. Or of the furious nurse when he returned. Her head rested on the sea's calm and burnished waters, her body sank into its welcoming warmth. She slept.

When Walter Burnleigh got the bad news thirty minutes later and tried to reach Michael, it was too late. Michael had been operating for some time and the operating room was incommunicado.

And no one could find Katherine Blair.

"Wonderful . . . the most exciting novel in my field to come along since Straub's **GHOST STORY.**"
—Stephen King

THE CEREMONIES

T.E.D. Klein

Summer.

A time of hope for Sarr and Deborah Poroth and the other stern fundamentalists in the small farming community of Gilead, New Jersey. A time for giving thanks. A time for celebration. A time of love for graduate student Jeremy Friers, vacationing on the Poroth farm, and the girl he is rapidly losing his heart to—Carol Conklin.

A time of growing terror . . . for other celebrations have also begun. Rites not performed for centuries. Rituals designed to release horrors from the earth itself . . . rituals that require the lives of two innocent, unknowing sacrifices—Jeremy and Carol.

Summer has come. And the Ceremonies have begun.

Don't miss THE CEREMONIES, available July 1, 1985, wherever Bantam Books are sold.

DON'T MISS
THESE CURRENT
Bantam Bestsellers

☐	23994	**THE OIL RIG #1** Frank Roderus	$2.95
☐	23117	**RAIN RUSTLERS #2** Frank Roderus	$2.95
☐	24499	**VIDEO VANDAL #3** Frank Roderus	$2.95
☐	24595	**THE TURNOUT MAN #4** Frank Roderus	$2.95
☐	24706	**THE COYOTE CROSSING #5** Frank Roderus	$2.95
☐	23952	**DANCER WITH ONE LEG** Stephen Dobyns	$3.50
☐	24257	**WOMAN IN THE WINDOW** Dana Clarins	$3.50
☐	24363	**O GOD OF BATTLES** Harry Homewood	$3.95
☐	23823	**FINAL HARBOR** Harry Homewood	$3.50
☐	23983	**CIRCLES** Doris Mortman	$3.50
☐	24184	**THE WARLORD** Malcolm Bosse	$3.95
☐	22848	**FLOWER OF THE PACIFIC** Lana McGraw Boldt	$3.95
☐	23920	**VOICE OF THE HEART** Barbara Taylor Bradford	$4.50
☐	23638	**THE OTHER SIDE** Diana Henstell	$3.50
☐	24428	**DARK PLACES** Thomas Altman	$3.50
☐	23198	**BLACK CHRISTMAS** Thomas Altman	$2.95
☐	24010	**KISS DADDY GOODBYE** Thomas Altman	$3.50
☐	25053	**THE VALLEY OF HORSES** Jean M. Auel	$4.95
☐	25042	**CLAN OF THE CAVE BEAR** Jean M. Auel	$4.95

Prices and availability subject to change without notice.

Buy them at your local bookstore or use this handy coupon for ordering:

SPECIAL
MONEY SAVING
OFFER

Now you can have an up-to-date listing of Bantam's hundreds of titles plus take advantage of our unique and exciting bonus book offer. A special offer which gives you the opportunity to purchase a Bantam book for only 50¢. Here's how!

By ordering any five books at the regular price per order, you can also choose any other single book listed (up to a $4.95 value) for just 50¢. Some restrictions do apply, but for further details why not send for Bantam's listing of titles today!

Just send us your name and address plus 50¢ to defray the postage and handling costs.